"I thought it b
for being so ru

"You've got nothing to be sorry about as far as I'm concerned," Samuel said quietly. "You were saying what you felt and that's a good thing."

"You're not concerned about our parents trying to make us marry?"

"Don't you see, Willow? The more we push against it, the further that increases their desire to match us together."

Willow was a little disappointed at his words. She would've been pleased for him to say instead how much he admired her and that she was a kind and caring person—just like his mother had told her that he'd said of her.

"If we pretend to go along with it, though, there comes a time when it must all come to an end. So how does that work?" Willow asked.

He wagged a finger at her. "I haven't quite figured that out yet."

Willow smiled at him. He was quite funny, to her surprise, and he had a wicked smile.

"Perhaps if we put our heads together, we can come up with a plan," Samuel said and grinned…

Samantha Price is a bestselling author who knew she wanted to become a writer at the age of seven, after her grandmother read her *The Tale of Peter Rabbit*. Though the adventures of Peter started Samantha on her creative journey, it is now her love of Amish culture that inspires her. Her writing is wholesome with more than a dash of sweetness. Samantha lives in a quaint Victorian cottage with three rambunctious dogs.

AMISH WILLOW

Samantha Price

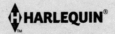

Recycling programs
for this product may
not exist in your area.

ISBN-13: 978-1-335-45492-8

Amish Willow

HARLEQUIN®
www.Harlequin.com

Printed in U.S.A.

Chapter One

"Here they are, Willow."

Willow ran over to the bedroom window and stood next to her sister, Violet. They both looked down at the Troyers, who were coming to dinner—again. It seemed the Troyers were always over and they always brought their only son, Samuel.

"It's obvious both sets of parents have put their heads together and are planning on you and Samuel marrying," Violet said in a tone that Willow knew meant she thought it was funny.

Willow crinkled her nose and pushed some strands of hair back under her prayer *kapp*. She took a moment to respond as she studied Samuel tying the reins of the buggy horse. "It's not that they'll force me; they can't do that. They just think that I'll grow to like him if he keeps coming here. That's their plan. Now that you're getting married, it seems they can't wait for me to go as well. I thought they'd want me around."

Violet laughed. "Don't be silly."

"I'm not. Why else would they keep having them here to dinner? We've heard all their stories before and

Samuel just sits there looking bored. I bet he wishes he were elsewhere, just like me. It wouldn't bother me if I never got married. Anyway, I've told *Mamm* I'll never be in love with Samuel so there's no point in them being here all the time."

Violet gasped. "You didn't tell me that!"

"I thought I did."

"Nee."

"I meant to. *Mamm* just said that love grows and develops after marriage. To me, that seems a huge risk to take. What if love never happens and I become stuck with a man I don't like? Anyway, it seems safer to remain unmarried than to take that risk."

"You'll change your mind."

"I doubt it."

"What about love?" Violet asked.

"Humph. That's right. Love should just happen by itself. It can't be forced like they're trying to do. They think nothing of love. I don't think *Mamm* and *Dat* could've been in love when they married. They don't understand anything about it."

Years ago, Willow remembered, she'd had a little crush on Liam Hostetler, but that was a long time ago. Willow figured that true love would be like that crush, but with more intensity and more butterflies in the tummy. Back when she'd had that crush on Liam, she could not wait to get to *schul* every day just so she could see him. Willow knew that true love was something that lasted and not a crush that one simply outgrew, but she still expected those sorts of feelings.

Both girls continued watching their guests until Samuel and Mr. and Mrs. Troyer walked into their *haus*.

"I suppose we'd better get back down there to help

Mamm again," Willow said. "She'll already be cross with us and wondering where we are."

Willow found the Troyers boring, and the same for their son. She talked to them only to be polite, and because she had no choice. Willow always tried to do what was right.

Just as they were about to head down the stairs, Willow stopped and whispered to her sister, "Marrying Samuel is simply out of the question."

Violet gave her a little shove. "I know that. Talk about it later. *Mamm* will be furious we're not there to help."

Willow headed down the stairs first.

The girls greeted the Troyers in the main living room and then left to help their *mudder* with the last of the dinner preparations.

Once they were in the kitchen, Willow whispered to Violet, "He's too tall and too thin."

"Mmm." Violet agreed. "But he kind of looks handsome today with his hair all windswept and now that his skin is darker from the summer sun."

"*Nee*, he doesn't look handsome, not at all," Willow said, shaking her head at Violet's bad taste in men. In the past, Willow had had some enjoyable conversations with Samuel, but more recently he had become silent and sullen with her. Now he wasn't friendly at all; he didn't even try to make conversation anymore.

Willow and Violet placed the bowls of food in the middle of the table so everyone could help themselves. Their mother put the last of the cutlery on the table.

"Can I do anything to help?" Mrs. Troyer appeared in the kitchen.

"*Nee, denke*, Louisa. We've just finished."

Willow's *mudder* called everyone to take their places at the dinner table. The three men left the lounge room and headed into the kitchen. As soon as they were all seated, silent prayers of thanks for the food were given.

The meal was Willow's favorite, roast chicken and roasted vegetables, with mounds of creamy mashed potatoes. There was coleslaw, which Violet had made earlier in the day, and both girls had worked together to make cheesecake for dessert.

Willow's father was the first to speak. "This looks *wunderbaar*, Nerida," he said to his wife.

"*Denke*, John," Nerida said, smiling at her husband.

"*Jah*, it does, Nerida," Samuel's mother said.

"*Denke*, but Willow did most of it. She's a *gut* cook."

Both Mr. and Mrs. Troyer smiled at Willow. Willow smiled back, but in her heart she was annoyed with her mother. This was what *Mamm* always said when the Troyers were there. She'd helped a little but it was a far stretch to say she'd done it all.

It did not go unnoticed by Willow that Samuel barely looked at her that night. While everyone heaped food on their plates, Willow studied Samuel. Was he as uncomfortable as she was with both sets of parents meddling in their lives? He never spoke much, in her experience, so it was hard to say. All Willow knew of him was that he was good at volleyball and ice-skating, and not much more. Life would be unbearable if the two of them were forced to wed. She would run away before she'd allow that to happen.

Maybe the Troyers want to marry into a large family since on Dat's side there are lots of cousins, and the Troyers only have one son and no daughters.

Willow wondered why the Troyers were keen for their boy to marry her. She was only seventeen and far too young to marry, in her opinion. Although, some of the women in the community married that young.

Dat cleared his throat and ran his hand down the side of his long gray beard. "Willow and Samuel, we're having this dinner tonight to discuss your wedding."

Willow nearly choked on the food in her mouth. She spat it out on her plate rather than attempt to swallow. "What?" Her eyes flew to Samuel, hoping he would help in her protest. He simply looked at her and looked away, apparently disgusted at the vulgarity of her table manners. She was not going to let him keep silent on the matter. "Samuel, didn't you hear what my *daed* just said?" She looked him in the eye, hoping he'd say something for once.

He shrugged his boring shoulders. "*Jah*, I'm happy to do what my parents want. I don't mind."

"You don't even like me." It was true and she had to say it so both sets of parents would hear the truth.

"Hush, Willow. Or I'll send you to your room." Her *daed* turned away from Willow and smiled at Mr. Troyer. "I'm sorry, Josiah; she's not usually like this."

"*Jah* I am. This is exactly how I am and I won't stand for nonsense. I'll choose my own husband. No one else I know has had a marriage arranged for them." Willow jutted out her bottom lip at her father in a defiant manner, which was against Willow's usually calm nature.

Violet, who was sitting next to her, dug Willow in the ribs. "Talk about it later, Willow. Not now."

Her *daed* pushed out his chair and stood to his full height. "Willow, go to your room now."

Willow stood up, pushed in her chair, and walked

quickly out of the room. Willow could feel her father's embarrassment at his youngest daughter speaking so disrespectfully to him in front of their guests.

Chapter Two

Closing her eyes, Willow hoped that the dinner would soon be over so the Troyers would go home. She would not be trapped into marrying a man who appeared disinterested in everything, including her. She'd have to run away, but where would she go? She had no money, no job, and certainly no skills with which to get a job.

Now sitting on the top step, she heard Mr. Troyer say, "The way I see it, the two of them could get married this next wedding season. What do you think, John?"

Her father answered. "*Jah*, that's what would be best. Soon after Violet and Nathan marry."

It was clear to Willow no one was on her side and no one even cared what she thought of the situation. The only person who understood at all was Violet, but she was in no position to be of any help.

Willow sat on the stairs listening while her parents talked to the Troyers about a wedding that would never take place. She had thought that her outburst at the dinner table might have put Mr. and Mrs. Troyer off the idea of her marrying their son, but it seemed they thought she was a good choice for some reason.

From Samuel's silence, he was just as disinterested as she, but most likely for an entirely different reason.

Finally, Willow heard the Troyers say goodbye. She hurried to her room, switched off the gas lamp by her bed, and sat by the window in the dark to study them as they left.

Samuel was first out the door, clearly showing his desire to get away from the house. He untied the reins and turned the buggy around so it was ready for his parents to get inside. As she studied his appearance in the moonlight, Willow had to admit that some women might find Samuel handsome, but why didn't he pay her any mind? As a woman, she considered herself his equal in attractiveness. Didn't he notice that?

When they were finally gone, Willow slumped onto the bed and turned her light back on. She knew her parents wouldn't berate her further that night about her behavior, preferring to leave it until morning.

A few minutes later, Violet came into her room with a plate of food.

"*Denke*, Violet. What am I going to do when you get married and I'm alone with them?"

"You shouldn't speak about them like that."

Willow sighed, "Yeah, but do you know what I mean? Why are they in such a hurry to get me married off?" She dug her fork into the creamy mashed potatoes. "*Denke* for this."

"You're welcome. They were trying to make me marry someone else. Don't you remember that?"

"*Nee.* If it didn't happen to me, I didn't take much notice."

Violet giggled. "Aunt Nancy and *Mamm* didn't want me to marry Nathan. They were trying to push some-one else at me."

"Do you think Aunt Nancy is behind this?"

Violet shook her head. "*Nee*, I don't. It's too clumsy. Aunt Nancy would work out something much better than the Troyers being here all the time."

"Anyway, they can't make me marry."

"No they can't," Violet agreed.

"I don't know what I'll do without you—when you're not living here anymore."

"I'm not getting married for a couple of months. So you'll have to put up with me until then."

"It seems almost like they're trying to make it a double wedding. They don't like me and don't want me around when you go. Don't you see that?" Willow asked.

"They love you. You're their *boppli*."

"Why are they trying to get rid of me then? I could understand if I was twenty-five or something, but I'm not even eighteen."

"They're doing what they think is best. They really like Samuel. He's got a good job and he's got men working for him now, including his own father. He's a hard worker, and he's a man of God."

"I don't see that there's anything special about him."

"He comes from a good *familye*."

Willow cut a piece of chicken and popped it into her mouth.

Violet shrugged her shoulders. "Do you want me to talk to Aunt Nancy for you and see if she knows what's going on?"

"*Nee!*" Willow shook her head. "I don't want to start

another argument between *Mamm* and her. And Aunt Nancy matched all her girls and probably the older boys too. She's more meddling than *Mamm* has ever been."

"Okay. What should we do?"

"I'm thinking of running away."

"You can't!"

"I'll go on *rumspringa*. Betsy has gone on *rumspringa* and she said I could come stay with her anytime."

"Maybe you should."

Willow ate another forkful of potato. When she'd swallowed, she said, "I don't really want to. I will if I have to, though, rather than marry someone I don't want."

Violet giggled. "I have a feeling the Troyers won't be over anytime soon with your outburst tonight."

"Good!"

Willow couldn't sleep that night. She tossed and turned, thinking of a plan to turn her parents off the idea of her marrying Samuel Troyer. Firstly, she had to figure out why they liked him so much.

Finally, figuring it would be best to speak to both parents together, she hurried downstairs early the next morning when she heard them at the breakfast table. Both of them turned and stared at her when she walked into the kitchen.

"*Mamm, Dat*, I'm very sorry about last night. I ruined the night and I feel dreadful about it and I'm sorry."

Her mother nodded and her father said, "Apology accepted, and you should also apologize to the Troyers."

Willow nodded. "I'll tell them as soon as I see them at the meeting on Sunday."

"*Nee*. You should go to see them today and tell them," her mother said while her father nodded.

Her father added, "*Jah*, make it a special visit so they can see you really mean it."

That was the last thing she wanted to do—the very last—but she couldn't tell her parents that. She was trying to calm them down, not whip them into a fury. "You're right. I'll visit them." She'd go in the middle of the day so both Mr. Troyer and Samuel would be at work. "Can I ask you why you think Samuel is a good match for me?"

"You've grown up with him."

"No more than anyone else, and he's not even my age. I don't even remember him at *schul*."

"He left *schul* to work. He's a capable man and he'll be a good provider. You need an older man because you're…"

"I'm what, *Dat*?"

"You're a bit immature and you tend to be a little gossipy."

Willow pulled a face and opened her mouth at what her father said. "I'm not!"

"Don't talk to your *vadder* like that, Willow."

"I'm not being rude; I'm just saying he's wrong."

"He's your elder," her mother said. "And your *vadder*."

Willow sighed. What was the point of trying to communicate with them? They never understood her.

"Your *vadder's* right. You listen in to what people say and then you tell other people what they said.

You've been like it all your life. What you need is a strong man to keep you in line."

Willow froze to the spot. This was not good. Now she really knew what her parents thought about her. She had to be smart about finding her way out of these intentions they had for her. "I didn't know I was like that. I should change."

"*Jah,* and Samuel is the man who'll change you."

Willow frowned at her mother. "Why?"

"You'll have a home. You'll be too busy with a husband and a family of your own to go sticking your nose into other people's business, and talebearing."

"Why him, though?" If she could find out why they thought Samuel was so good, that might be the key to changing their minds—either that, or she could always run away.

Her mother looked over at Willow's father, and he said to Willow, "You just have to trust us that we know best."

"Sit down and I'll get you some breakfast."

Willow sat down opposite her father. She had nothing left to say to either of them. Why couldn't they be supportive of her the way her friends' parents were with them? None of them were trying to force a marriage onto their daughters—it was unheard of.

"What time do you plan to visit the Troyers?" her father asked.

"I was thinking about eleven?"

"Okay. I'll make some cookies for you to take," said her mother.

"Sounds *gut. Denke, Mamm.*"

Her father drained the last of his coffee, and then kissed Willow and her mother goodbye.

When her mother placed a plate of pancakes in front of Willow, she sat down next to her. "I know you don't think Samuel is right for you now, but love grows. Love is not so much a feeling, but an appreciation. Love is giving to the other person and thinking of them more than you do yourself. You only truly know what love is when you are married, so no more outbursts. You'll thank us when you're married."

Willow stopped herself from rolling her eyes. She'd heard it all before. "I understand that, *Mamm*, but what I don't understand is that Violet got to pick Nathan, so—"

"Nathan just happened, and at the time I thought she'd be much better suited to someone like Benjamin."

"So you were wrong?"

"*Nee.* She could've been just as happy with Benjamin."

Her mother had an answer for everything. "Violet's wedding isn't far away," Willow said.

"What does that have to do with anything?" her mother asked.

"It's just that maybe you should concentrate on that before you start looking for a husband for me. Don't you want me around or something?"

Nerida narrowed her eyes at her daughter. "Now you're just being unreasonably rude. Nancy is helping with the wedding and she's had six of her *kinner* married. One by one they married, and now they're all happy and their families are growing."

"Don't you and *Dat* want me to be in the *haus* with you when Violet's not here anymore?"

"Of course we do. But we want what's best for you

and your future. We're not even thinking about ourselves. You should know that."

Willow remained silent and continued to eat her pancakes, not wanting to anger her mother further by telling her that she felt otherwise.

"I'm visiting Nancy today, so I'll take you to the Troyers' and collect you on my return."

Willow stared at her mother, unsure of what to say. That idea meant she'd be stuck at the Troyers' for ages. "Okay…" she eventually said, knowing that no matter how she tried to come up with some alternative, it wouldn't be acceptable to *Mamm*.

"That means you better hurry up with those cookies or they'll still be hot when we get there."

"I thought you said you were making the cookies for me."

"I can't do everything! I've got washing to do this morning."

"Jah, Mamm."

While her mother did the washing outside, Willow made the cookies. Violet woke up just as she was in the middle of cutting them.

"What are you doing?"

"What does it look like I'm doing? I'm making cookies. And I'm going to take them to the Troyers."

Violet laughed. "You're *what*?"

"I apologized to *Mamm* and *Dat* for last night, and they said I should apologize to the Troyers. Or maybe it was my idea, I can't remember. Either way, I do owe them an apology, and I'm taking cookies to them."

"That's nice of you. Leave some for me."

"There'll be plenty. *Mamm* is taking me there on her way to visit Aunt Nancy."

Violet pinched off some cookie dough and popped it in her mouth. "You could be there for ages."

"That's what I'm afraid of. Are you going with *Mamm*?"

"I could."

"You're not working today?"

"*Nee*, not today. I'm seeing Nathan later tonight."

"You could go with us then, and hurry *Mamm* up if she's taking too long."

"Okay." Violet moved to the end of the kitchen and placed the teakettle on the stove to heat. Then she asked, "How do you know Samuel will be home?"

"That's just it. I'm hoping he won't be. That's why I told *Mamm* I want to go at eleven. He should be at work."

"Not if he comes home for lunch."

"Oh, Violet, don't even say that! It never crossed my mind."

"I don't know why you didn't think of that. A lot of men come home for the midday meal."

"I'll have to hope that he doesn't. Because I've seen enough of him, especially after last night."

"He's really not so bad, but I can see how you're upset with everything."

"Good! I'm glad you can see how horrible it is. I would've thought *Mamm* and *Dat* had enough to do, what with your wedding and everything. We'll probably get a lot of visitors staying here at the *haus* and that means *Mamm* will put us to work when she goes into her usual pre-visitor cleaning frenzy."

"She will, but not until about a week before."

Violet stayed in the kitchen while Willow cut out, baked, and then decorated the cookies.

"You're not making them taste too good, are you?" Violet asked.

"I don't think it would make a difference. Everyone would pretend they tasted good anyway, and bad cookies won't get me out of their stupid ideas about marrying me off. Mrs. Troyer will probably just try to take me under her wing and teach me how to make cookies properly."

"Yeah, and that will make *Mamm* annoyed and then the two of them will have a falling out."

"Hmmm, that's not a bad idea," Willow said with a sly smile, which made Violet giggle.

Chapter Three

"Knock on the door and we'll wait here to see if she's home," Willow's mother said.

Willow picked up her plate of cookies, climbed down from the buggy, and walked to the Troyers' front door. She glanced back at her mother and Violet who were waiting in the buggy.

Mrs. Troyer opened the front door before she reached it.

"Willow, how lovely to see you again so soon."

"Hello, Mrs. Troyer. I hope you don't mind if I stay awhile, while my mother is visiting her sister."

Mrs. Troyer waved to the others in the buggy. "I'd love you to stay. Come in."

Willow looked back at her mother's smiling face as she turned the buggy around. When Willow stepped inside the house, she could hear the buggy horse clip-clopping back down the drive. "I've come to say I'm sorry for the way I behaved last night." She held the plate up. "I've brought you cookies."

"Cookies? Lovely! Come through to the kitchen and I'll make us *kaffe* to go with them."

She'd completely ignored Willow's apology, and Willow wondered if she hadn't heard. Did that mean she'd have to say it again?

Willow sat down at the table while Mrs. Troyer put the teakettle on the gas stove. "I don't get many visitors," she said when she turned around. "I suppose I would if I had more *kinner*." She sat opposite Willow. "More *kinner* would mean more people coming and going."

Willow nodded.

"We wanted more, but it wasn't *Gott's* will that we have more than one. That's made us very grateful for Samuel."

"*Mamm* only had the two of us. Aunt Nancy had six, as you know."

"Twins are in your family. They must be, because of Tulip and Daisy."

"*Jah*, except my twin cousins are Lily and Daisy."

"My mistake—that's right, Lily and Daisy. So you could easily have twins, Willow."

Jah, someday when I'm older and married, Willow felt like saying, but she was there to apologize, not to speak her mind further. "I haven't given that a great deal of thought." Since they seemed to be getting along okay, Willow thought she'd ask some questions. "Can I ask you why you and Mr. Troyer think I'd be a good match for Samuel?"

"Samuel's shy and he's not married, and we're just trying to give him a helping hand. He likes you."

"Does he?"

"You look surprised."

"I am. He…well, I mean…he doesn't seem to. It's

just that he's a lot older than me. Don't you think some-one older would be more suited for him?"

"*Nee.* Is that why you came here today, Willow?"

"I came to apologize for my rudeness at the evening meal last night."

"And you're not interested in my son?"

When Willow looked into Mrs. Troyer's blue eyes, she didn't have the heart to tell her she wasn't inter-ested in Samuel.

"I can't really say; I don't know him very well."

"Ah, we'll have to do something about that."

When the water boiled, Mrs. Troyer jumped up to pour it. Running through Willow's mind was the thought that if she found someone for Samuel, some-one older and more suited, then the pressure would be off her. "Mrs. Troyer, has Samuel ever been interested in a girl—has he dated before?"

Sitting back down with a teapot on the table, she shook her head and said, "Only you."

"Me?"

"*Jah,* I told you that."

"He's only been interested in me?"

Mrs. Troyer nodded.

Willow's stomach churned. How could parents be so disconnected from their children? "Samuel hardly knows me." *Besides, the people who know me think I'm a bit of a brat and a busybody,* she felt like saying. What could Samuel see in her? She was no beauty, and she didn't have a brilliant mind. Not that men seemed to look for brilliant women. She was plain old Willow. When she grew older she was sure she'd develop some remarkable qualities, but now she felt she was like a flower before it bloomed—she was just a bud. No one found a plain green bud adorable.

"Between us women, Samuel talks about you quite a lot. Oh dear! I said I'd make *kaffe*, but I made hot tea instead."

Willow gave a little giggle as she took the cover off the cookies. "Hot tea's fine." As Mrs. Troyer poured the tea, Willow asked, "What kind of things does he say about me?"

"He likes the way you're so friendly with everyone. At each Sunday meeting you get around and talk to nearly everyone. He says that shows you're kind and caring."

Willow bit into a cookie. Her parents thought she was a gossipy talebearer for doing just that. They didn't think she was talking to everyone because she had redeeming qualities. Maybe Samuel saw things in her that other people didn't see? Now Willow's insides were glowing instead of churning. She'd have to think about Samuel a little harder, rather than discard him because of their parents' doings.

"What upset you so much last night, Willow?"

"I don't like being pushed into things, and I think I'm too young to get married. I hadn't even thought about it seriously yet."

"Never?"

"*Jah*, that's true. I have thought about it, in general I mean, but I haven't told myself it's time to get married or anything like that. I don't even have a job and I have hardly done anything in my life."

"You don't need to have a job."

"I know that, but I think I'd *like* to have a job and

get to meet people and that kind of thing while I'm still young."

"What's to stop you from getting a job?"

"Nothing." When Mrs. Troyer continued to stare at her, Willow admitted, "I guess I'm a little nervous." She meant *lazy and I haven't bothered to do anything about it*, but she couldn't tell Mrs. Troyer that.

"My *bruder* is looking for a girl to do some office work for him in his lumberyard. Do you think you could do that?"

"What would I have to do?"

"I don't know. He just said office work. His last girl left and he hasn't been able to find anyone reliable."

"Is that Mr. Hostetler, Liam's *vadder*?"

"*Jah*. David Hostetler is my *bruder*."

Liam was the boy she'd had a crush on back in *schul*.

"They're coming to dinner tonight and I'll put in a good word for you."

Willow's mouth fell open. "Would you do that— really?"

"*Jah*." Mrs. Troyer sipped her tea.

"*Denke*. That's nice of you."

"And then you go see him tomorrow. I'll tell him you'll be there then to talk with him. And you can both see if the job will be a good fit for you."

"That's exciting." Now Willow was happy that she'd come to see Mrs. Troyer. "I'm so glad I came to see you today."

When they were nearly at Nancy's house, Violet said, "Will you stop the buggy, please? I'll walk from here. I need some exercise."

"Why?"

"I'm feeling fat."

"Don't be silly. Is this because of the wedding and knowing you'll soon be married?"

"I guess so. I want to be trim."

"You look fine."

"Please, *Mamm*?"

Nerida rolled her eyes and moved the buggy off the road to let her climb out.

"*Denke*. I'll see you soon, *Mamm*."

Nerida started the horse moving again, heading to her sister's house.

Once she arrived, she opened Nancy's door and walked right in. "Nancy? Where are you?"

"I'm here, in the kitchen baking."

Nerida breezed into the kitchen, said hello to her sister, and promptly filled up the teakettle. "Cup of tea?" she asked Nancy, quite used to making her sister's home her own.

"*Jah*, please. Just give me whatever you're going to have."

While Nerida waited for the kettle to boil, she sat down at the kitchen table, watching her sister.

"How did last night go?" Nancy asked.

Nerida told her sister what she'd been planning for Willow. "And things couldn't have gone any worse. Willow jumped up and ran out of the room. I was so embarrassed. I don't think I've ever been more embarrassed. I didn't know what to do, and poor Samuel! He seemed to take it well. He just sat there looking as if women ran away from him every day of the week."

Nancy giggled. "Perhaps they do."

"You're the one who started this, you know, by suggesting John and I think about him for Willow."

"And I still do think that he's the best man for her by far, but I can't say I like the way you two have gone about things."

Nerida's face soured. "And I suppose you could've done better?"

"Judging by what happened last night, I couldn't have done much worse." Nancy pushed the dough to one side, washed her hands, and then sat down at the table with her sister.

"Does this mean I've ruined things?" Nerida asked.

"I can't tell you that, but what I can say is that you have to pull back and stop now that she's on to you. She'll just fight against it. You have to act as if you don't care whether she marries him, or anybody else."

Nerida shook her head. "She won't believe that."

"It doesn't matter if she believes it or not, that's what you have to do. If you'd taken my advice in the first place, you wouldn't have kept inviting them over for dinner. And did John say what you told me he was going to say? That you four parents were going to discuss their wedding?"

Nerida nodded.

"Well there you go. How thoughtless of him." Nancy threw her hands up in the air. "And is that when she ran out?"

"A few less-than-pleasant words were said before that."

"The only way to fix it is to do what I said. After all, I got all my—"

"*Jah*, I know. You got all six of your *kinner* happily married off. And it was all due to you."

Nancy sensed a little tension in the air. "I'm sorry, that was a bit prideful. I'm only trying to help."

A knock sounded on the door.

"That would be Violet. She had me stop the buggy so she could walk a little. She thinks she's fat."

"Come in," Nancy called out.

Violet walked into the kitchen and greeted her aunt.

Nancy asked, "What did you want to walk part of the way for? Are you trying to lose weight for your wedding or something?"

"It doesn't hurt to get a bit of exercise," Violet said, glancing at her mother.

"You certainly don't need to lose any. Nathan doesn't care about your weight," Nerida said.

"*Mamm*, you're saying that as if I'm very big. I'm not that big but I just want to lose a little bit of weight so I can feel more comfortable."

Nerida rolled her eyes.

"What were you talking about?"

Nancy said, "Your *mudder* was just telling me about how Willow was upset at dinner last night."

"*Jah*, she feels she's far too young to marry, and she hardly knows Samuel at all, so I don't blame her for getting upset."

"You two are always sticking together," Nerida said.

"Only because that's what I really think. I'm not saying that just to stick up for her. It's a big decision to marry someone. And she wants to make that decision on her own, not have it made for her. Can't she do that?"

"Your *vadder* and I are just a little worried about it, that's all."

Violet said, "Just let her grow up and do things in her own time. That's my advice. She'll be okay."

Nerida looked at Violet and then at her sister. "I

suppose you're both right. John and I put too much pressure on her last night. We'll have to do what you suggested, Nancy."

"And what's that?" Violet asked.

"Nancy said we shouldn't do anything at all."

"And I quite agree with that," Violet said. "And, in that regard, perhaps we should go and rescue Willow now? She's already been there long enough to make her apology."

"You're right." Nerida stood. "Let's go."

Chapter Four

Just as Mrs. Troyer and Willow finished their tea, they heard a buggy coming toward the house.

"That was fast," Willow said, standing up. "Aunt Nancy must have been away from home."

Mrs. Troyer stood up, too, and looked out the window. "It's Samuel, home for the midday meal. He's a bit early."

"Oh, I thought it was *Mamm* coming back to fetch me."

"I didn't notice the time slipping by. Will you be a dear and go out and tell him lunch will be another twenty minutes or so?"

"Of course." When Willow walked out of the house, she was a little embarrassed that she was there. And if he liked her so much like his mother said, why was she only just learning about it now? And from her, instead of from him? Samuel certainly didn't act like he was keen on her.

He was out of the buggy and leading his horse closer to the barn when he looked over and saw her. "Well, this is a nice surprise, Willow. What are you doing here?"

"I came to visit your *mudder*."

He looked around. "Where's your buggy?"

"My *mudder* left me here while she and Violet visit Aunt Nancy. She's getting me soon."

"Not too soon, I hope," he said with a smile.

"Your *mudder* says to let you know the midday meal won't be ready for another twenty minutes. It's my fault; I distracted her."

Samuel secured the reins.

Willow continued talking, because he was barely talking at all. "I thought it was best that I come over here and apologize for being so rude last night at dinner. So, I'm sorry to you as well."

"You've got nothing to be sorry about as far as I'm concerned. You were saying what you felt and that's a good thing."

"You're not concerned about our parents trying to make us marry?"

"Don't you see, Willow? The more we push against it the further that increases their desire to match us together."

Willow was a little disappointed at his words. She would've been pleased for him to say instead how much he admired her and that she was a kind and caring person—just like his mother had told her that he'd said of her.

"If we pretend to go along with it, though, there comes a time when it must all come to an end. So how does that work?" Willow asked.

He wagged a finger at her. "I haven't quite figured that out yet."

Willow smiled at him. He was quite funny, to her surprise, and he had a wicked smile.

"Perhaps if we put our heads together, we can come up with a plan," Samuel said as he started walking toward the porch. He indicated that Willow should sit on one of the porch chairs, and then he took the other.

"That's a good idea, as long as they don't work out what we're doing." Willow sighed. "I don't know why they just can't leave me alone. I'm far too young to get married."

"You don't think I am?"

She looked into his blue eyes to see if he was joking and she couldn't tell. He seemed serious. "You have to be a good ten years older than me. I don't even remember you being there when I started school so that must—"

"I'm only twenty four. Not ten years older than you, like you say. Only about seven. Ten years would make me an old man; nearly as old as your *vadder*."

Willow giggled. "Well, I'm glad you're not taking the whole thing too seriously."

"I know I want to get married someday, so I guess that's the true reason I went along with it. And, as you said, I'm such an old man…"

Willow felt her cheeks warm and she looked away. "I suppose everybody wants to get married, but doesn't a person have a right to choose when and to whom?"

"That's exactly right, Willow. It's not nice that they've taken over from us."

"Well, you're an adult. They all just think of me as a child. Why don't you say it's not what you want?"

He tipped his hat back slightly and scratched his head. "I tend to prefer to stay away from trouble, and I'm not good when people nag me. *Mamm* will nag me and go on and on talking about it. I guess I find it easier to just go along with it."

It sounded like he was a man with no backbone and Willow did not want a man like that. She wanted a man who knew what he wanted and went after it no matter what anybody said. Not a man who was just going along with things that other people wanted.

"Why are you looking so sad?" he asked.

"I'm not sad. I'm worried. I don't like people forcing me to do things either, but I'm not just gonna go along with it and hope something works itself out. We have to come up with a plan."

He crossed his arms over his chest and leaned back. "Let's hear it."

"I haven't thought of anything yet, except I know that we need to come up with a plan. Why don't you think of something?"

"How about I tell my parents that I'm interested in someone else?" he suggested.

"Who?"

"I won't say who, I'll just say someone else. It won't be fair to expect you to marry me when I like this other woman."

"That makes sense. So, do you like someone else?"

"If I did, I wouldn't have gone along with my parents this far."

"So that's a no?"

"That's a no." He laughed at her. "You're very forceful."

"I hope that's a good thing."

"Depends."

"Depends on what?"

He looked down. "Nothing."

"It must be something."

He looked up at her with a look on his face as though he really liked her. To cover her embarrassment, she said, "Will you really tell your parents you're interested in someone else?"

"If that's what you want me to do."

Willow nodded. "I would be grateful if you did." Willow hoped it could be that easy.

"I'll tell them soon."

"You can't tell them tonight. You've got people stopping for dinner."

"Who is it? You?"

"*Nee*, it's your *Onkel* David and his family."

"Well, I'll tell them soon, anyway."

"*Denke*, Samuel. I really appreciate you doing this."

"I really had no idea what my parents had in their minds at first. I was just as shocked as you last night when your father said the thing about being there to discuss our intended marriage."

"You didn't seem that shocked."

He chuckled. "I was. Believe me, I was. Too shocked to even look shocked, I guess."

"Why did you think you were coming there for dinner all the time? Violet and I were already suspicious that your parents and mine were trying to match us together. I thought you would have seen that."

"Not really. My *mudder* doesn't have many close friends and I just saw that she was getting close with your *mudder*."

As they talked, Willow found herself attracted to him, and she didn't want to be. His skin was tanned and his blue eyes stood out against his dark skin, the whites of his eyes matching the whiteness of his teeth.

* * *

Willow's attention was taken by a buggy. She turned to see that it was her mother and Violet coming to fetch her. *What rotten timing!* Maybe...maybe she didn't want Samuel to tell his parents he liked someone else, but it was too late now to say anything further to Samuel.

"Here they are to fetch me. I'll just say goodbye to your *mudder*."

"Okay."

She stood and opened the door, leaning inside. "Mrs. Troyer, *Mamm's* here to collect me."

Mrs. Troyer came out of the kitchen. *"Denke* for stopping by, Willow. I'll talk to my *bruder* tonight, and I'll tell him you'll come into the lumberyard tomorrow."

"Wunderbaar, denke. What time do you think I should get there?"

"He'll be there all day."

"I'll go early."

Mrs. Troyer smiled and Willow saw that she had the same color eyes as Samuel. Would Mrs. Troyer regret recommending her to her brother when Samuel told his mother he liked someone else? Willow couldn't say anything now; all she could do was thank Mrs. Troyer again and leave. That's exactly what she did. On her way to her mother's buggy, she turned back to Samuel. "Goodbye, Samuel."

"Denke for stopping by. *Mamm* gets lonely here by herself all day."

"Does she?"

He nodded. *"Jah.* That's why I come home for lunch."

Willow continued walking to the buggy while

thinking how kind Samuel was to be concerned for his mother like that.

As soon as Willow got into the buggy, her mother said, "How was your visit?"

"We had a lovely time. I'm glad I went. We talked about me getting a job and she said she's going to talk to David Hostetler, her *bruder*, who owns the lumberyard. She said he has a job there for someone to do office work."

"You never told me you wanted a job," Violet said.

"It's something I've just been thinking about."

"I could've asked around at the markets for you."

"I don't think I want to work at the markets. I want somewhere quieter to work. I don't like to be around a lot of noise and a lot of chatter."

"That's only because you want to be the one doing all the chattering," her mother said.

Willow ignored the jibe, and took great delight in saying, "Another thing I found out is that Samuel likes someone else. We had a talk and he's going to tell his *mudder* and *vadder* soon."

"Is this some scheme you have cooked up, Willow?"

Willow gasped. How could her mother know her so well? "What do you mean, *Mamm*?"

"Did you put Samuel up to this?"

"*Mamm*, how could you say such a thing?"

"Answer me."

"*Nee*, he told me himself. He likes someone else, not me. His parents didn't even bother to check with him if he liked someone else. So I don't know what last night was all about, and all the other times the Troyers have been over. We haven't had anybody else in the community over so much. Not anybody else at all, even if they're not in the community, come to think of it."

Violet turned around and looked at her. Willow knew she'd have to tell Violet the truth because the expression on her sister's face told her that she was highly suspicious. Her sister knew her all too well.

"Anyway, I'm excited about the job. She said to go there early. No, wait a minute. She said go there anytime tomorrow because her *bruder* is going to be there all day, but I said I'd go there early. I can borrow the buggy, can't I?"

"Of course, if it's for a job."

"Denke."

"If you ask me, Samuel was looking at you as though he liked you. He had a twinkle in his eyes and he found it hard to look away. It was sweet. I think he likes you, but you don't like him and you made him say to his parents that he likes someone else. You cooked up this whole thing, didn't you, Willow?"

Willow was disappointed that she was so transparent. But the complete truth of the thing was that it wasn't her idea. The idea, the actual suggestion, had been Samuel's.

"Samuel and I were just talking about our parents and he said he was shocked when the subject of marriage came up and I said I was too. And then we talked some more, and he said he was interested in another woman. His parents had never even asked him."

"And why would he offer you that information unless you said you weren't interested in him?"

"He's not just going to marry me when he's interested in someone else, *Mamm*. Don't you think so, Violet?"

"Willow does have a point."

"And he's going to tell his parents what you just told me?" *Mamm* asked.

"*Jah.* That's right."

When they arrived at the house, Willow's mother said, "I feel a headache coming on. You girls can un-hitch the buggy and fix dinner tonight. I'm going to lie down in bed."

"*Jah, Mamm,*" both girls said in unison.

Once their mother was inside, Violet stared at Willow. "Okay, tell me what really happened."

"It was just like I told *Mamm.*"

"I know there was a lot more to it than that. So tell me. You've always told me everything so don't stop now."

Willow unhitched the buggy while telling Violet exactly what had been said.

"And the thing is, after getting to talk with him one-on-one, I kind of like him now."

"It's a bit late for that now. You were so rude to him, Willow. The poor man would've been really em-barrassed."

"He didn't seem embarrassed at all. We were just laughing and talking away. He is so easy to talk with, come to think of it. And his eyes are a lovely blue color, just like the sky on a clear summer's day. And his skin is dark but it doesn't look like leather. I bet it's soft to the touch."

Violet led the horse into the paddock while Willow pulled the buggy further into the barn.

"What did you do at Aunt Nancy's, Violet?"

"Talked about the wedding and what food we would have. Well, after Aunt Nancy told *Mamm* that she shouldn't have tried to match you with a man in the way that she did."

"*Gut!* I wish I could've been there."

"You can come next time. We are meeting again next week to talk about the same thing." Violet shook her head.

"What's the matter?"

"I think that *Mamm* and Aunt Nancy just like weddings. You're the last wedding they'll have any real say in."

"Well I won't get married for some time, then, and that will give them something to look forward to," Willow said.

"Maybe they don't see things that way."

"Well it's my life and not theirs. They have lived their lives and now they should let me live mine."

Violet giggled. "Now you know how I felt when they were trying to match me with Benjamin."

"I knew how you felt all along. But I didn't want you to like Nathan at first, either."

"*Jah*, you made that quite clear. You were rude to him."

Willow smiled. "*Jah*, I was, but I really like him now. And I'm sorry I misjudged him."

"That's good. I'm glad you like him; he'll soon be your *bruder* by marriage. I hope you get that job at the lumberyard. What will you have to do there?"

Willow shrugged her shoulders. "I don't know. She just said office work."

"Who said that?"

"Mrs. Troyer. She said the job's for office work, and I'm not quite sure what that is. Probably working with computers and things like that. If I get the job, it might make *Mamm* and *Dat* think of me as more grown up and they'll stop trying to run my life. They'll see I'm my own person with my own mind and not someone to be pushed around."

"I know what you mean. I hope we're not like this with our *kinner* when we have them."

"That's a long way off into the future—for me, at least. If you turn out like *Mamm*, Violet, I'll tell you to stop being so bossy."

"And I'll tell you the same."

"Did I give *Mamm* a headache?" Willow asked.

"Probably."

"I feel bad about that, but what can I do? It wouldn't have worked out with Samuel anyway. It's embarrassing. I hope no one finds out they were trying to force me to marry him."

"I'm sure Samuel won't be telling anyone."

"His *mudder* seemed quite convinced that he likes me."

"That's not so good. Hopefully, they won't be over for dinner so much now. Not that I've got anything against them, but I've heard Mr. Troyer's stories over and over again about how he used to fish and swim in the creek with all his brothers and what a good time they had jumping into the water from the rope swing."

Willow agreed. "I know the stories by heart. I could tell them myself."

Nerida stayed in bed the rest of the day and only came down for a dinner of meatballs, sauerkraut, and mashed potatoes.

When they were all seated around the table, Willow's father looked directly at Willow, and said, "It seems we've made a mistake about Samuel."

Willow nodded, hoping her father wasn't angry.

He added, "We'll say no more on the matter."

"Are you feeling better, *Mamm*?" Violet asked.

"*Jah*, I am."

"You girls need to help your *mudder* more around the *haus.*"

"We will, *Dat*," Violet said.

"I'm going to see about a job tomorrow, *Dat*," Willow said.

"*Jah*, I heard about that. Will it be full time?"

"I'm not certain. Anyway, Violet only works part time, so she'll still be around the house when I'm not. Until she gets married, anyway."

"I won't be far away," Violet said.

"You'll have your own household to take care of, and you'll be doing that."

"I can still—"

"Willow will help out here."

"*Jah*, of course. I always do more than my share." Willow was tempted to ask who would help around the place if she'd gotten married like they'd planned, but thought better of it.

"I don't know if I like the idea of you working in a lumberyard, but I won't stop you if that's what you want to do."

"*Denke, Dat*. I never thought I'd work in a place like that, but I'll be happy if I get the job."

"You'll get the job if it's *Gott's* will," her mother said.

Chapter Five

Willow drove the buggy away from home the next morning, feeling good to be seeing about the job. Being the youngest in the family, it was rare she got a chance to drive the buggy alone and she enjoyed the peace and quiet. The November morning was frosty even though the last few days had been unseasonably warm. She breathed in the dew-scented air and enjoyed the chill that greeted her skin.

She pulled the buggy up next to the lumberyard and secured her horse amid the sounds of woodcutting saws in the distance. The Hostetlers' lumberyard was the biggest in the area and that was the only thing she knew about it. She'd been there only one or two times before, when her father was doing a building project.

After she had taken a deep breath, she walked into the office. Mr. Hostetler was sitting behind a large desk. He looked up when she walked in.

"Good morning, Mr. Hostetler."

"Willow. Good morning. I've been expecting you. My *schweschder* said you'd be stopping by today. Have a seat."

Willow sat on the opposite side of the desk. "*Jah*, she was kind enough to tell me that you might have a job."

"And you're here to tell me that you're the right person for that job?"

"I hope so. Let me start by saying that I'm a fast learner, but I have never had a job before and someone would have to show me what to do and then I'll be sure to be very good at it."

He laughed.

"The main thing I want is someone to sit here behind this desk and take phone messages. That would be the first priority. I don't want to be stuck here on the phone when I've got so many other things to do. After you learn how to answer the phone inquiries, and you learn the pricing system, then my bookkeeper might be able to show you how to get the paperwork ready for her."

"I'm sure I'd be able to do that. And do it very well."

"I'll tell you what. What if we both try the job out for a week? You see if you like it and I'll see if I think you're a good fit for the job. You'll be paid for the week, of course."

"Do you mean it? I've got the job?"

"What you've got is a tryout, for a week."

"That's what I meant. And if I do a good job you'll keep me on?"

"That's right. When can you start?"

"Willows! What are you doing here?"

There was only one young man who called her Willows, and that was Liam Hostetler.

Willow turned around to see him. He took off his hat and ran his hand through his golden-brown hair. His eyes were nearly the same color as his hair, only darker.

"I'm here about a job."

He smiled. "You'll be working here?"

His father stood up. "We're giving Willow a trial for a week. Starting tomorrow, if she's able."

"Oh, *jah*, tomorrow would be fine. More than fine. Shall I start at nine?"

Mr. Hostetler tilted his head. "We start at seven thirty around here."

"I'll be here by seven thirty, then. Is there anything else you need from me today, Mr. Hostetler? Do I need to tell you anything else?"

"I can get all the other information from you tomorrow. I'll see you bright and early tomorrow morning."

"I'll be here, and *denke* for the opportunity."

He smiled, puffing out his ruddy cheeks. "Goodbye, Willow."

"I'll walk you out," Liam said. "How did you get here?" Liam asked once they were outside.

"I've got my buggy," Willow said.

"So you'll be working with us?"

"You work here too?"

"*Jah*. I thought you knew that. Isn't that why you wanted the job, Willows?"

Willow stopped still and looked at him. "*Nee*, not at all."

"Relax! I'm only joking."

"Oh."

"Since when did you get so serious?"

"Over the last two days," Willow said, which caused him to laugh. But she wasn't joking. Finding out that her parents wanted her to marry someone was more than enough for her to lose her sense of humor.

"Are you still going on *rumspringa*?" Willow asked.

"Yeah, I might. I'll have to wait and see. What about you? We could run away together."

Willow giggled. "I've only just got the job."

"So what? If you get the boot, you'll find another job with your personality."

"Not when I've got no experience. I need this job."

"No one needs anything except love, that's what makes the world go 'round." Liam grabbed her hand and Willow pulled away.

"Stop. People can see."

"Let's go behind your buggy so we can hold hands."

"Nee." She laughed at him being so cheeky.

"I'll wear you down yet, Willows."

"We'll see. And stop calling me Willows. That's not my name. If you don't stop it, I'll start calling you Liams."

He chuckled. "I'm glad I'll be seeing you every day."

"What do you do here?"

"A bit of this and a bit of that."

"Tell me what exactly. I'll have to know, since I'll be working here."

"It's hard to explain. You have to work here to understand what I do. I'll tell you tomorrow afternoon, after your first day."

"Okay. *Gut.*" Willow climbed up into the buggy.

"I'd like to see more of you, Willows. Sorry, I mean Willow."

"You will. I'll be here tomorrow. And then at least for a week, unless your *vadder* gives me a permanent job and then I'll be here all the time."

"That's not what I meant."

"I have to go."

She moved the horse and he grabbed the horse's cheek strap.

"Where are you going?" he asked.

"I've got things to do and you've got to do some work. Your *vadder's* probably watching you right now."

Liam glanced over the horse's back, peering toward the office. "I'll see you tomorrow, Willow."

"Bye." Willow trotted the horse away, pleased that Liam had been flirting with her. It made her feel good about herself to know that he liked her.

A black car drove by her, and it was coming from her house. It was an odd sight to see because they didn't know any *Englischers*. Through the dark windows, she saw that an older man with glasses was driving. *He looks like a doctor*, she thought.

Excitement about Willow's new job overtook her curiosity over who was in the black car. She'd find out who he was a bit later. Being too excited to unhitch the buggy, she left it and hurried inside to tell her mother the exciting news.

"I got the job," Willow called out as she ran into her house.

Her mother came out of the kitchen. "You did?"

"Jah."

Willow hugged her mother.

"That's *wunderbaar* news."

"It's a week's trial, and if I do good, he said he'll give me the job permanently."

"Oh, you'll have to do well."

"Jah, I will. I've always been good at everything I do. And I'm not being prideful, it's true."

"The job's made you happy, so that's good."

"I think I'll like it there. I have to answer the phone and take messages, and probably take orders over the phone, and then I'll learn to do the paperwork. I like to learn new things. Liam works there too, but I didn't know that. I knew he worked for his *vadder*, but I didn't think he worked at the lumberyard. I thought he did building work."

Her mother sat down.

"Who was that in the black car just now?"

"Just a doctor. I went for a check-up the other day and I left something at the office and someone was kind enough to drive it to me."

"What did you leave?"

Her mother looked away. "It's not important. Now that you're home, I'll have a lie down."

"You're not sick or anything, are you, *Mamm*?"

"Just tired. That's all. Don't forget I'm getting older."

"*Jah*, but you're not that old. You're not sixty or even fifty or anything. Who else will I talk to if you go to bed?"

"Talk to yourself." Her mother walked toward the stairs.

"Have you been sleeping okay at night, *Mamm*?"

"I've had a bit of trouble sleeping at night."

"Probably because you've been sleeping during the day. If you didn't sleep in the daytime, then you would be able to sleep better at night."

Nerida put her hand to her forehead. "Willow, your constant chatter is hurting my head. Have you noticed that you speak about three times as much as a normal person? Sometimes it's hard to take."

"Sorry, *Mamm*. Do you want me to bring some tea up for you or anything?"

Her mother shook her head. *"Nee, denke."*

Then something struck Willow like a bolt of lightning in a deserted cornfield. Her mother was dying! That's why she was so anxious for Willow to get married. And that was also why her father asked Violet and herself to do extra chores and help their mother. It wasn't because he thought that they weren't doing enough, it was because their mother was ill and possibly even dying.

All the pieces of the puzzle fell into place in her mind, and Willow wondered how she could have missed it. And she'd seen that doctor driving away from the house!

Her mother was normally full of energy and now she often had an afternoon nap. And only old people had those, or very young people. Or sick people. She would have to tell Violet as soon as she came home.

Willow sat on the couch and cried. What was she going to do without a mother? Did her mother want grandchildren before she passed? How soon was she going to die? That must be it; she wanted grandchildren from both her and Violet before she died.

Should she marry someone just to give her mother grandchildren? If that's what her mother wanted, she'd feel awfully selfish if she didn't give her that gift. After all, *Mamm* had given her the gift of life. This was one sacrifice she could make for her parents. The only trouble was she had to get to Samuel and stop him from telling his parents that he liked somebody else. She would match herself up with Samuel. He wasn't too bad. In fact, she'd really enjoyed their conversation outside his home.

She scribbled a note to her mother and left it on the

kitchen table so she would find it when she woke. Then she went outside, glad she hadn't unhitched the buggy when she'd gotten home. She hoped Samuel hadn't told his parents already.

Samuel and his father had a business that made gazebos, with Samuel gradually assuming the management position. Their showroom was close to the Hostetlers' lumberyard. Could she talk him out of telling his parents that he was interested in someone else? He might become angry with her for changing her mind. She didn't know what to expect.

When she turned into the land that the business was on, she saw Samuel in the distance. Since it was very hot, she parked the buggy in the shade of the building and hurried over to Samuel.

He caught sight of her and walked to meet her. "Hello, Willow. What brings you here?"

"You haven't told your parents you're interested in someone else yet, have you?"

He grimaced. "Don't be mad at me, but I completely forgot."

"Phew."

"You're pleased?"

"Jah."

"I'm confused. Now you *don't* want me to tell my parents I like someone else?"

"That's right. Not yet."

"When do you want me to do it?"

"I'm not sure. Can you just not do anything until I talk to you again?"

He frowned at her. "What's this all about?"

She couldn't tell him that she was going to have to marry him to give her mother a grandchild before she died. She couldn't hurt him like that. If she had to marry him, she'd pretend to love him and maybe she might fall in love with him one day. "I can't say."

He smiled. "I'm pleased you changed your mind. We should go out together and celebrate—maybe go out to dinner?"

"Maybe. We're very busy at home at the moment organizing Violet's wedding. Maybe after that?" Willow mentally patted herself on the back for her fast thinking. By Violet's wedding, she would've gotten down to the bottom of things and found out what her mother was dying from and how long she had to live.

"Too busy for dinner? Surely you have to eat."

"That's true."

"Why don't I take you out to dinner tomorrow night?"

"I'm starting my new job tomorrow and I'll be a bit tired, most likely."

"You're working now?"

"*Ach jah.* I just got a job today at your uncle's lumberyard. It's really a trial for a week, so I'll have to make sure I do a really good job."

"What about Saturday night? There'll be no meeting the next day because it's the second Sunday and you won't have work the next day."

She was trapped and couldn't think of anything on the spot. "Okay, that would be nice. I'll look forward to it."

"Me too. Perhaps our parents knew something that we didn't."

So much for Mrs. Troyer telling her he liked her. She clearly had made that up or had been mistaken. "You never know."

"Did you come all the way here just to ask that?"

"Jah."

"We do have a phone here. You could've called."

"It would have been a strange thing to talk about over the phone."

He laughed. "That's true."

"I better get home to *Mamm.* She'll be wondering where I've gotten myself to."

"I'm glad you stopped by."

Willow nodded, then turned and walked to the buggy. Aunt Nancy was her next stop. If something was wrong with her mother, and if she'd told someone, it would be her sister.

Chapter Six

Willow opened the door and poked her head into her aunt's house. "Aunt Nancy?"

"Come in, Willow."

Willow followed her aunt's voice and found Nancy in the kitchen.

Nancy stared up at her from the kitchen table. "You're here by yourself?"

"*Jah.* I thought I'd stop by because I was just passing on my way back from somewhere."

"Sit with me. How's your *mudder* been?"

Willow sat down. "Why? Do you know something?"

Nancy frowned. "About your *mudder*?"

"*Jah.*"

"All I know is that she's been very tired and very stressed with this wedding coming up."

"It's not that stressful, is it?" Willow asked.

"You'll have visitors staying with you, and I'll have visitors staying here, and that's a lot besides all the organizing that's got to be done. I'm helping her with that because I've done it a few times before." Nancy gave a little laugh.

"Would all that make her so tired?"

Nancy drew her eyebrows together. "How tired are we talking?"

"She sleeps for a long time every afternoon."

"Isn't she sleeping through the night?"

"That's what I asked her and she said she's not sleeping well at night."

"That'll do it. Don't worry so much."

"Do you think that's all it is?"

"I'm certain that's all it is."

Willow didn't tell her about the black car she'd seen or her other suspicions. Nancy genuinely had no idea, and that must've been how her mother wanted things.

"I got a new job, well, it's my first job, and I start tomorrow at the Hostetlers' lumberyard."

"That's *wunderbaar*. I didn't know you were even looking for a job."

"It happened quite quickly when I was talking with Mrs. Troyer yesterday."

"*Jah*, that's right, her brother owns the lumber yard."

"It's only a week's trial at first, but I'm sure I'll do well and they'll want to keep me. Anyway, I was just passing by, and now I better get home and get the evening meal cooked."

"*Denke* for stopping by. Don't worry about your *mudder*, she's okay. And she'd need extra sleep if she's not sleeping at night."

"Of course, that makes sense. I thought she might be dying. Are you sure she's okay? I saw a doctor, or a man who looked like a doctor, in a black car driving away from the house."

Nancy's eyes widened. "That's odd."

"I know."

"Did you ask her about it?"

"*Jah*, she said she left something at the doctor's office when she was having a check-up and they brought it to her. She never goes to the doctor."

"What did she leave?"

"I asked, but she brushed it aside."

Nancy shook her head. "I wouldn't worry about it."

"You're not keeping her illness from me? I won't tell if they've asked you not to say anything."

"*Nee*. She's fine. Stop worrying. If there was anything wrong she would've told me, and she hasn't said a thing."

"Phew! That's good. I should head home." Willow leaned forward and kissed Nancy on the cheek. "See you later."

"Bye, Willow."

When Willow got home there was no sign of her mother, so she raced up to the bedroom and found her just getting out of bed.

"Where have you been, Willow?"

"I went out for awhile. Why? Were you calling me?"

"*Jah*, I wanted to remind you to put dinner on."

"Okay, *jah*. Here I am now and I was just about to do that."

"*Denke*. Violet doesn't get home till later tonight. Nathan is collecting her from work and then they're going out to dinner somewhere. So it's just the three of us."

As Willow walked down the stairs, she knew it was going to be lonely in the house after Violet got married. It had always been the two of them doing everything together. It was already a little strange to see her spending so much time with Nathan. Willow had taken some time to get used to Nathan and had to admit she had been wrong about him. Although she and Nathan didn't get along particularly well even now, she knew he was good for Violet.

Willow waited up that night until Violet came home. In an excited whisper, she told her about the new job and then informed her about the black car and her other suspicions.

"I've noticed that she hasn't been eating very much lately. Do you think she could really be sick?" Violet also whispered so their parents couldn't hear.

"That's the only thing I can think of that make sense."

"What are we going to do?"

"I'll have to get married, because I know *Mamm* wants a grandchild before she dies." Willow sighed.

"You said that you're not ready to be married."

"I'm not, but what else can I do?"

"I don't know. How are we going to find out for certain if she's sick?" Violet asked.

"*Dat* would have to know. If he hasn't told us by now he's not going to, and I went over to Aunt Nancy's house today and asked her. I'm sure she doesn't know anything about it. She said *Mamm's* just tired because of all she has to do for your wedding."

Violet suggested, "Maybe if we got married at the same time, *Mamm* wouldn't have to go through two weddings at two different times."

"Get married on the same day?"

Violet nodded.

"That would be working too fast. You think someone would marry me on the same day as you? That's only weeks away. That reminds me, Samuel asked me out to dinner on Saturday night."

"And you said yes?"

"I did."

"That's good, but you're right; it probably would be too fast. He's not going to ask you to marry him the first time you go out with one another. So, you like him now?"

"I liked him a bit better when I talked to him alone, without anyone around. That's the first time I've talked to just him. When anyone's around he just shuts up." Willow yawned. "I'm so tired. I better go to bed because I'm gonna wake up and get to work early."

"I'm not working tomorrow."

"That's good. I can take the second buggy."

"Try not to worry about *Mamm*. We'll get to the bottom of it. Don't rush out and get married until we know for certain if she's dying or what."

Willow agreed.

Willow felt grown up driving herself to work the next morning and she had made certain she woke up in plenty of time to be early. When she stopped in the parking lot, she saw Mr. Hostetler and Liam arriving in their buggy, and they pulled up beside her.

After they exchanged hellos, Willow tended to her horse and then walked into the building with her new boss and his son.

"How are you feeling?" Liam asked.

"A little nervous and excited."

"Don't worry about anything. *Dat* will show you what to do and then Maureen is coming in a bit later."

Mr. Hostetler said, "Maureen is the bookkeeper I was telling you about."

"The first thing we need to show Willow is where the coffee is kept," Liam said with a smirk.

Mr. Hostetler shook his head. "You and your coffee. Surely you can make your own."

"Not if there's someone else to make it for me."

Willow said, "I don't mind making coffee."

"See, she doesn't mind," Liam said to his father.

"Okay, show Willow where the break room is and then you can come back, Willow, and I will get started with your training." Mr. Hostetler sat behind his desk.

"Would you like a cup of coffee, Mr. Hostetler?" Willow asked.

"I wouldn't mind a hot tea. White with one."

Willow headed to the break room with Liam.

"Don't be nervous."

"I'm not nervous."

"You look it."

"That's just excitement, not nervousness."

He laughed. "Whatever you say."

They walked into the break room and Liam showed her where everything was. There was a large, complicated-looking electric machine that made coffee using beans, not the instant coffee that Willow made at home.

Liam talked her through it. "I was spending so much money on coffee from the shops every day that I figured it would be cheaper to buy this machine, and the coffee tastes just as good."

Willow liked the sound of that. She liked a man who was careful with his money and who wasn't wasteful.

She followed all of his instructions while he watched, and then she handed his coffee to him.

He took a sip. "Perfect."

"Good. I just have to remember how to do it again."

"You'll need plenty of practice."

Willow made Mr. Hostetler's tea and left Liam alone in the break room.

"Here you go. I don't know if I put enough milk in it," she said, handing the tea to her boss.

"It looks fine to me. *Denke*, Willow." He stood up and moved away from behind the desk. "This desk is yours now, since you'll be answering the phone and taking the orders and the messages."

While he drank his tea, he told her what to say when she answered the phone, showed her the price list of all the goods, and then handed her a calculator. "Are you good at math?"

"Very good."

"That's great, but for now, all buyer inquiries can be put through to Jenny, and you'll have to learn from her. If any customers have difficult questions, put them on hold and page someone. You'll meet the team this morning."

A few hours into the job, Willow was pleased that it wasn't as hard as she had thought it might be. She was told she could have her lunch between twelve and one, and then she remembered the lunch that she had brought and left in the buggy. At noon, Maureen said she'd watch the phones and Willow headed outside to get her lunch. When she turned to head back, she was face-to-face with Liam.

"Are you going to go inside?"

"I was planning to."

"On a beautiful day like this? Come for a walk with me." He held his own sandwiches up for her to see. "There's a nice little park not far from here. You don't have to stay on the premises when you're on a break."

"Okay, that sounds good. You're right, it is a beautiful day."

The park was only a couple hundred yards away.

"Do you like working with your *vadder*?" Willow asked as they sat down on a wooden seat in the park.

"I haven't worked anywhere else so it's hard to judge. I suppose it's all right, and it'll be mine one day. That's extra incentive to do a good job." He laughed and unwrapped his sandwich. "How are you liking it so far?"

"I like it very much." Willow bit into her sandwich.

"Have you thought more about running away with me?" he asked with a straight face.

"I haven't given any thought to running away, with you or anybody else."

He smiled. "I'll have to get you to change your mind."

"You do a lot of talking about going on *rumspringa*, but so far I haven't seen any action."

"Ouch! You've got your claws out today. Meow."

"They're always out, so watch out."

He laughed. "I will."

"Why do you want to go on *rumspringa* anyway?"

"So I can do all the things I've never been able to do, of course. Nearly everyone goes on *rumspringa*."

"I'm not interested because I know I'll come back here anyway, so what's the point?"

"When you're older, you might regret not having spread your wings, and then it'll be too late."

"I'll keep that in mind. *Denke* for the advice, Liam."

"I might have to go on my own."

"I think you will."

Liam pulled a face and Willow giggled.

"I really like the sound of your laughter."

Willow turned to look at him and he held her gaze, making her feel uncomfortable. She bounded to her feet and her second sandwich fell from her lap.

He picked it up and shook off the dirt. "I didn't want to make you upset."

"You didn't," she said.

"This is no good anymore." He threw the sandwich into a clump of grass.

"I should get back inside and learn some more things, since this is my week's trial. I want to make a good impression."

"You've already made one on me." He smiled and gave her a wink.

"The lumberyard isn't yours yet, so you're not the one I need to make a good impression on." She started walking back to the office and he walked after her.

He caught up with her, and said, "Do you want one of my sandwiches, Willow?"

"*Nee*, I'm fine, truly. I've had enough."

"Would you like me to take you out for dinner one night? Maybe Saturday?"

"Why, because you made me drop my sandwich in the dirt?"

He laughed. "I'm not sure that it was my fault. *Nee*, because I want to see more of you."

"I can't on Saturday night." Right then, they reached the office.

"Are you busy on Saturday night then, Willows?"

She turned around to face him and frowned. "It's Willow, Liam, and yes, I am."

"I hope you're not going out with another man."

He said it as a joke, as though he didn't think she would be. She didn't laugh, and then she took her place behind the desk.

"Willow, are you going out with another man on Saturday night?"

"You say 'another man' as if we're dating or in some kind of relationship."

"Don't play with words. Are you dating someone?"

"No, but I am going out with someone on Saturday night, and I don't want to say who it is."

He straightened up and looked cranky. "I'll find out."

"Don't make a fuss. It's nothing. Now I need to get back to work."

Just then Mr. Hostetler walked into the office and stared at his son. "Don't you have something better to do, Liam?"

"I'm still at lunch, *Dat*."

"I don't see you eating anything, son."

"Okay, I guess lunch is officially over."

When Liam left the office, Mr. Hostetler said to Willow, "Was my son bothering you?"

"*Nee*, Liam and I are good friends."

"He can be a little overwhelming at times."

"Everything's fine."

Chapter Seven

Willow's parents were delighted when they found out she was going out with Samuel on Saturday night.

"I knew you'd like him," Willow's father said while she was waiting for Samuel to collect her.

"I hope you can understand that I need to know whether I like him," she countered.

He nodded, saying nothing more.

Willow's mother sat on the couch just smiling while Willow paced up and down. Normally her mother had sewing or crochet work in her hands, but this evening she had nothing. "Come here," she said.

Willow walked over and her mother straightened her dress, and then said, "Tie the strings of your prayer *kapp* together."

"Do I have to? No one does," Willow said.

"I think it looks better. Please yourself. I can't force you to."

"She's fine like that," her father said.

Willow sat down next to her mother. "How are you feeling tonight, *Mamm*?"

"Why do you keep asking me that? Do I look sick or something?"

"*Nee*, you don't. You look lovely. As pretty as ever."

Her mother chuckled. "I'm just hoping you get along with Samuel and I'm glad that you are going out with him, and you're giving him a chance."

"That's all we ask," her father added.

"It sounded like a whole lot more than that the other night. You were talking about discussing our marriage."

"We didn't know you'd have such a bad reaction to that."

Willow's eyebrows flew upward. "It's not every day someone is told they have to marry someone."

"He's a good man, and sometimes parents do know best," her father said.

"We shall see."

"He's a bit older than you, he's mature, and he'd look after you."

Willow looked into her mother's eyes, knowing *Mamm* wanted her daughters to be secure when she died and didn't want that burden to lie on her husband. "I'll be okay, *Mamm*. And if I don't marry soon, I can look after myself. There's no hurry for me to marry, is there?"

"There is a chance Samuel won't wait around forever. He could marry someone else."

"He could've done that at any time, and he hasn't," Willow pointed out.

"That's him now," her father said.

Willow looked out the window. "Yes, that's him. Do I look all right, *Mamm*?" She smoothed her hands down her dress.

"You look beautiful."

"Denke, Mamm."

"Don't forget your shawl," her father called after her.

Willow hurried out of the house, lifting her shawl from the peg at the back door as she went past. She approached the buggy and Samuel jumped down and tried to help her.

"I don't need any help. I'm fine."

"It seems quiet at your house tonight."

"Violet has gone out with Nathan and it's only my parents there."

Once they were both in the buggy, he turned the buggy around and headed back down the drive.

"How are you doing at your job?"

"Good. Only a few more days to go of the trial, and I love it."

He glanced at her. "That's good when you can find work you enjoy. Liam works there, doesn't he?"

"Jah."

"How are you getting along with him?"

"Good. We went to *schul* together. Do you know him very well?"

"He's my cousin."

"That's right." Willow giggled. "I forgot."

This was Willow's first real date out alone with a man and she was excited. She tried not to remind herself of the fact that her parents liked him so much. She didn't want to be forced into anything. But it wasn't his fault that they both had pushy parents.

Soon they were in town and Samuel stopped the buggy in a nice area where there were many restaurants.

"Where are we going? What restaurant?"

"You'll soon see."

"Have you been there before?"

"I have."

Willow wondered if he had been there before with a girl. She hadn't heard his name attached to any girls and she was sure she had heard all of the rumors circulating; his name definitely hadn't come up.

She got out of the buggy as soon as it stopped.

After he secured the horse, he said, "It's up this way." His head nodded up the street.

They walked along the sidewalk together and Willow felt even more on edge.

Once they'd been shown to a table in the dimly lit restaurant, and had been handed menus, Samuel leaned close to Willow. "Okay, now that we're here, you can tell me what's up with you. Why the sudden change? You suddenly like me now, or what?"

Willow knew he was referring to her asking him not to tell his parents he was interested in someone else like they'd planned. "It's just that… It's hard to say, really."

"You seemed pretty anxious for me not to go ahead with telling my parents the story about my liking someone else."

Willow looked down at the empty table setting in front of her. She couldn't tell him that she suspected her mother was dying and she was willing to sacrifice herself to marry him to make her mother happy in her dying days. Her cheeks grew hot. He would've thought she liked him. When she looked up, she saw him frowning at her.

"Whatever it is, you can tell me. I know you're not madly in love with me. So what is it?"

"It's just that I thought we could see how things go and then take things from there."

"I can see you're not going to tell me," he said.

"Maybe because there's nothing to tell."

He chuckled, and then said, "Whatever it is, I'm glad that you've come to dinner with me tonight. Let's just concentrate on enjoying ourselves."

"That sounds like a very good idea." Willow felt the knot in her stomach relax.

The waiter returned and they quickly made their choices from the menu, and when the waiter left, there was silence between them.

Samuel seemed nice and gentle. Maybe she could fall in love with him if she knew a little bit more about him.

"Tell me some things about yourself," she said, fiddling nervously with the knife and fork in front of her.

"You know I'm an only child and I don't have a lot of relations. There are the Hostetlers on my *mudder's* side and there are plenty of them, but there aren't many on my *vadder's* side."

"And you get on with them all okay?"

"I'm probably closer with people who aren't my relations. Liam's my closest cousin in age and he's quite a bit younger than I am. And that's probably why we were never that close."

Not wanting to talk about Liam, she asked, "So what do you want for the future?"

"I'm happy if things stay pretty much the same as they are now except that I'd like a *fraa* and *kinner*. I want a happy home full of the laughter of children. I suppose that's because there was only me in my family. I would like to have as many *kinner* as *Gott* gives me."

Willow hadn't given too much thought to how many children she wanted.

"How about you?" he asked.

"I guess I would be happy with just one or two. I guess whatever happens happens."

After they'd had about twenty minutes of getting to know one another, their meals arrived.

Willow stared at his baked salmon. "That looks delicious."

"Do you want a taste?" he asked.

"Do you mind?"

"Here, I'll cut some off for you." He cut a portion of his fish and put it on her plate.

"Do you want some of my steak?"

He shook his head. "*Nee, denke.* I don't eat a lot of red meat."

"Why not?"

"I prefer chicken or fish."

Willow popped the salmon into her mouth and it melted like butter. "Mm, that's delicious."

He laughed. "Do you want some more?"

"*Nee*, but *denke*. I've got plenty to eat here."

When they finished eating, he took a sip of his ginger beer. "Willow, you have the most beautiful eyes."

She looked at him and could see that he was being genuine, that he was not just trying to flatter her. *"Denke."*

"I'm trying to decide what color they are."

"I know some people say they're brown and some people called them green. Sometimes they look like a bluish green, so I'm told."

"Whatever they are, they're lovely."

"Yours are nice too. I've always loved blue eyes. Your mother has the same blue eyes as you."

"I guess that proves I'm not adopted," he said with a laugh.

"Did you once think you were?"

"It's crossed my mind from time to time. But my mother has too many stories of when she was expecting me and the birth and everything for her to be lying about it."

"She told you about the birth?"

"I'm afraid so. It was more information than I cared to know."

Willow put her fingertips over her mouth and giggled. "My *mudder* won't even talk about that kind of thing to me and Violet. She says it is just something we women have to go through. I mean, if I'm going to have to go through it one day, I would like to know a bit about it first. Maybe I'll have to talk to your *mudder*."

He smiled. "She'd probably like that very much."

"It must've been hard for her, wanting other children and not having them. I imagine it would have been very frustrating for her."

Samuel nodded. "She had a couple of heartbreaking miscarriages before I was born. She mourned, and people didn't understand. They just told her to try again."

"Sometimes people have to go through something to fully understand it. That would've been devastating for her. I hope that never happens to me."

"I hope it never happens to you, too."

Willow looked at the shirt he was wearing. "Does your *mudder* sew your clothes?"

He looked down at them, and when he looked back up at her, he asked, "What's wrong with them?"

She giggled. "I didn't say there was anything wrong with them. I just asked if she made them."

He lifted up the collar and looked down at it. "*Jah*, she does. Do you think I should buy some new clothes from a store?"

"*Nee*, they look fine. I was just asking, that's all. Why would your parents want you married? Don't they want you to stay around?"

He shrugged. "They've probably had enough of me by now. I'm well and truly too big for the nest and they're pushing me out to make more room for themselves."

Willow laughed. "Like two birds in the nest. You've gotten bigger than both of your parents and they need you gone."

He smiled. "That's right."

He was indeed physically bigger than both of his parents. At around six feet four inches tall, he towered over both of them. "Considering how tall you are, are you really sure you're not adopted?" she asked with a laugh.

"*Jah*, I'm sure I'm not. Have you ever wondered if you were adopted?"

"*Jah*. Don't you wonder if that's what all children think about? My mother wanted more children, too, because her sister had six and she only had the two of us. Just between you and me, my mother always wants to do everything like her sister. But if she ever heard me say that, she wouldn't be too happy."

"Her *schweschder* is Nerida—no, wait, that's your *mudder*. Her sister is Nancy Yoder?"

"That's right. Nancy Yoder. I really like *Ant* Nancy and *Onkel* Hezekiah. They're two of my most favorite people in the world, apart from my own family, of course." Willow sighed. "I don't know what I'll do when Violet gets married. We are very close. Well, a bit less close now since she's been spending most of her time with Nathan."

"Things in life are always changing. We have to adapt."

Willow slowly nodded. "I guess so."

"One thing I like about you, Willow, is that you're always bubbling over with happiness and always talking. You're a very cheerful person to be around."

Willow smiled at another compliment, and she was certain again that it was genuine.

After a nice dinner and two desserts, which they shared, Samuel drove Willow home. She decided she definitely liked him more now that she knew him better. Perhaps she could fall in love with him and that would make everyone happy—perhaps even herself.

When they stopped outside her house, she got out quickly so there wouldn't be an awkward moment where he might try to say something romantic, try to hold her hand, or lean in for a kiss on the cheek.

"*Denke*, Samuel. I had a lovely time."

"Perhaps we could do it again soon?"

"I'd like that." She turned and hurried into the house. As soon as she got inside, she realized she had left her shawl in his buggy. She opened the door to go back and get it, but he was already halfway down the driveway. After she closed the door behind her, she headed toward her bedroom.

"Willow."

She whipped her head around at the sound of her sister's voice from the living room.

"What are you doing up so late?" Willow asked.

"Waiting for you, silly. How did your date go?"

"It was my very first date."

"I know. That's why I'm waiting, so you can tell me how it went." Violet pushed her glasses further up her nose.

Willow sat down and told her all about her time with Samuel and what they had talked about.

"It doesn't sound like a very interesting conversation," Violet said.

"It was, though. We kind of talked a little bit about everything—even silly things. I think I like him."

"'Like' as in like, or 'like' as in you might see a future with him?"

"The last thing you said."

Violet's face lit up. "That's good. I can see the two of you together."

"Really?"

Violet nodded.

"Well, this is the first time I'm hearing that."

"I thought he was too old at first, but maybe that's a good thing for you."

Willow frowned at her sister. "Does everyone think I'm immature, or something? Even you?"

"*Nee.* It's not that. It's just that you're very chirpy and he is quiet, in a dependable way."

Willow thought for a moment about what Violet said. "I feel I could trust him, and he is very reliable. And that's a good thing in a man, I'd reckon."

"Have you had any more thoughts about *Mamm*? Do you really think she is dying?"

"I haven't found anyone to tell me she is. Aunt Nancy didn't seem to know anything about it. Why haven't *Mamm* and *Dat* said anything?" Willow asked.

"They wouldn't. They wouldn't want to worry us."

"What do we do?"

"We just have to live our lives and keep our eyes open," Violet said.

"I don't even want to think about what would happen if she wasn't here anymore." Tears flowed out of Willow's eyes. "If something happened to her, I don't think I would want to live anymore."

"Shhh. They'll hear you. We'd have to, Willow. We'd have to carry on without her," Violet whispered.

Willow sniffed. "She can't be dying too soon because she's planning the wedding."

"So that means she's got weeks and maybe months. Perhaps a whole year," Violet said. "Anyway, we need sleep. It's Sunday tomorrow, there's no meeting, and we should both enjoy the day of rest with *Mamm* and make the most of it."

Willow agreed and both sisters headed upstairs to bed.

When there was no meeting, on every other Sunday, those Sundays were very much days of rest. They couldn't do anything that resembled work or chores, so Willow's family normally slept late and then had a simple brunch, a breakfast and lunch combined, at mid-morning. In the afternoons, her parents normally went visiting while Violet and Willow visited their friends. Since Violet had become engaged to Nathan Beiler and went with him on Sundays, Willow went her own way and visited her own friends.

This Sunday, Willow and Violet had decided to spend time with their mother. While their parents were still asleep, they discussed how they would keep their parents at home that afternoon.

"What shall we do?" Willow asked as she shook cereal into a bowl.

"Tell them we want them to stay home today."

"They'll ask why."

"You could pretend you're sick. That's what you used to do for extra attention when you were younger."

Willow pouted. "I did not. I was really sick all those times."

Violet giggled. "I'm only teasing."

"It's no time to joke. We've gotta figure out how to get *Mamm* to stay home."

"We could just ask her."

"That's a good idea. I don't know why I didn't think of that. You can say because you'll be married soon you just want to spend the day with her, and *Dat* too, I suppose."

"I hope they haven't already arranged with someone that they're going to be stopping by."

"I don't think they would've."

Their mother walked into the kitchen. "*Guder mariye,* girls."

Willow turned to see that her mother looked ghostly pale. "Are you all right, *Mamm*?"

"I didn't get much sleep. Your *vadder* isn't feeling too well and he tossed and turned all night."

"*Dat's* never been sick."

"Well, he's not feeling too well today. I'm going to take him up some breakfast and a hot cup of tea." She looked between the two of them. "What do you girls have planned for the day?"

"Willow and I were just talking about that. We just wanted to have a quiet day sitting at home with you."

Their mother's face lit up. "With me?"

Violet nodded.

"That would be lovely. I can't think of anything nicer."

"I'll put the kettle on the stove, *Mamm*."

"*Denke*, Willow."

"What do you think is wrong with *Dat*?"

"He feels a bit hot. It's probably just some kind of a virus. I don't think it's anything to worry about. You girls better not go near him, though. I don't want you to catch anything. Particularly you, Violet, with the wedding coming up."

"But what about you, *Mamm*? You shouldn't be near *Dat* if he's got a virus, should you?"

"Someone has to look after him."

The girls helped their mother make a tray of breakfast to take up to their father.

When their mother left the kitchen, Willow said, "That turned out well."

"Except the part about *Dat* being sick."

"Yeah, that's not good."

The girls prepared breakfast for their mother, and she soon came downstairs with an empty tray.

"That's a good sign; he was able to eat it."

"I think he's feeling a bit better."

Their mother sat down and ate her breakfast of cereal. They never had a cooked breakfast on a Sunday, and it wasn't a day for any fancy cooking. The Sunday meals were either simple, or they'd been prepared the day before and could be easily reheated.

The girls spent the rest of the morning with their mother. They heard many interesting stories about when Nancy and she were younger. Nerida also told them that when she was a girl, all the clothes were washed by hand and wrung out through a hand wringer by turning a handle. There were no gas-powered washing machines. And all the clothes were hand sewn or sewn with a treadle sewing machine and very few people had the machines.

"It's so interesting to hear about the olden days," Willow said.

Nerida pulled a face. "They weren't the olden days. When my grandparents were young, *those* were the olden days."

"I didn't mean you were old, *Mamm*. You're quite a young *mudder* compared to some. Some mothers in the community are very old."

"There are no really old *mudders*; at a certain point, a woman can no longer have a child."

"*Jah*, we know all about biology, *Mamm*," Violet said.

Their mother continued, "Age is something that has never bothered me. You'll know when you grow older. You get more sensible as you see and hear a lot more things that happen around you, and you learn from that. Then there will come a point in time when you realize that what your parents told you was right. I never listened to my parents either. But now when I look back, I know that they were right in what they said about things."

Willow knew her mother was talking about her. Her

parents always thought Violet was the sensible one and she was just a brat. "I know you think I don't pay you and *Dat* any mind, but I do. I said I was sorry for my behavior the other night, and I even apologized to Mrs. Troyer and Samuel."

"I didn't mean anything by what I said, Willow. It was just a general statement."

"Ah, good."

"It must be well into the afternoon already. Aren't you going to see Nathan today, Violet?"

"*Nee.* He might come here later, but Willow and I want to spend the day with you."

Their mother smiled.

"I'll see him all the time once we're married," Violet said.

Willow added, "And that's not too far away."

"You don't have to remind me about that," their mother said. "There's so much to organize."

"I hope *Dat* will be all right," Violet said.

Their mother said, "I should go and check on him."

"Do you want another hot tea, *Mamm*?" Willow asked.

"You girls are spoiling me today."

"It's about time we spoiled you," Violet said.

When their mother was halfway up the stairs, Willow and Violet headed to the kitchen.

"Shall we ask her if she sick?" Violet said.

"We could, but what if she doesn't want us to know?"

"What if *Dat's* the one who's sick?"

Willow gasped. "What if we lose them both?"

"*Nee*, that couldn't happen. That couldn't happen at all."

"*Dat* still goes to work so it couldn't be him. *Mamm's* the one who sleeps all the time and looks pale."

Violet nodded. "That's true. I suppose you're right. We can't say anything." When they heard a buggy, Violet ran to the window. "That will be Nathan. Oh! It's not him. It's Samuel."

Willow joined her at the window. "Samuel?"

"*Jah*, Samuel. He must be here to see you."

"I didn't know he was coming." Willow was pleased to see him, and adjusted her dress and smoothed her hair back to make herself look attractive.

"You seem pleased that he's here," Violet said as Willow walked to the door.

"Not especially," Willow said, realizing just how happy she was that he'd stopped by. "Well, *jah*, I guess I am," she said when Violet gave her a pointed look. When Willow opened the door, she saw another buggy coming up the driveway. "Violet, here comes Nathan, too."

Violet quickly joined Willow at the door and the two of them waited for Nathan and Samuel. Willow glanced over when she heard her mother coming down the stairs.

"I'll put the tea on," their mother said.

"*Nee*, you're having a rest today, *Mamm*. We'll do everything."

"I should disappear upstairs so you girls can talk to your men by yourselves."

"*Nee*, *Mamm*, stay there."

The two men secured their horses and then headed to the house together. Violet went halfway to meet Nathan and Samuel continued to Willow.

"I hope you don't mind me stopping by, Willow."

"I'm glad you did. We were just having a quiet day at home." Willow leaned in and whispered, "It was getting a bit boring. I'm so glad you came."

A smile lit up Samuel's face.

The rest of the afternoon was spent with the two couples and Nerida talking over tea and cookies. Willow was pleased how well Samuel got along with everybody.

Chapter Eight

Willow was just about to go on her lunch break on Monday when she looked out the window of her office and saw Samuel's horse and buggy pulling into the lot. She wondered, *What is he doing here?* She'd only just seen him the day before. Then she realized that his business was making pergolas and of course he would've bought the wood from his uncle's lumberyard.

She was about to go ask if she could take her lunch early when the phone rang. The person on the line wanted to speak to Mr. Hostetler, so she was busy taking a message when she saw Liam walking outside. Now if only she could find one of the workers and have her answer the phone calls while she went to lunch… Otherwise she would have to eat lunch at her desk today. When she finished taking the message she paged one of the girls, but there was no response.

In the next moment, Samuel stood in the doorway of her office with her black shawl in his hands.

She stood. "You brought my shawl? I forgot all about it yesterday. I left it in the buggy on Saturday."

"I'm sorry, I didn't see it until this morning, otherwise I would've given it to you yesterday."

"Can I help you with anything, Samuel?" Willow heard Liam ask.

Samuel turned to face Liam. "*Jah*. I'm chasing up my order. Is it ready yet?"

"Your *vadder* said you didn't need that until the end of the week."

"That's right. Since I was stopping here, I thought I'd ask just in case it was ready early. Will it be ready then?"

Liam scratched his head. "It will be ready."

There was an awkward moment of silence while the two men looked at each other and then both looked at Willow.

"Do you get time for lunch, Willow?"

"Normally she does, but today the person who watches the phones during her lunch is not here. Is there anything else you want?" Liam asked.

"Do you mind if I have a quiet word with Willow?"

Liam's lips turned down at the corners.

"Make it fast." Liam disappeared, leaving the two of them alone.

"In a bad mood today, is he?" Samuel asked, moving further into the office.

"I don't know. This is the first time I've seen him today. Mr. Hostetler is away and I thought Liam was with him." Willow waved a hand in the air. "Don't mind him. He just gets bossy sometimes."

"*Jah*, I remember that from family gatherings. I just wanted to tell you I had a lovely time on Saturday night."

"I did too. *Denke* for bringing my shawl."

He passed it to her.

"I need it now that the days are getting cooler."

"Since you can't go out to lunch, do you want me to bring something back for you? There's take-out up the road."

"*Denke*, but I bring my lunch every day. We could have had something to eat together in the park, only I can't get away." Willow would've liked to talk to him again.

"I shouldn't hold you up. I'll see you again."

"Okay, bye."

He walked toward the door and turned around. "What about tomorrow night? Can I pick you up from your *haus* after work?"

"Um, tomorrow night? I think that will be fine." Willow smiled at him.

A bright smile appeared on his face, and his blue eyes twinkled. He gave her a wave and then walked out of the office.

As soon as Samuel's buggy headed away from the lot, Liam bounced into her office. "I heard that! Don't tell me you're interested in him?"

"*Jah*, I am. Why were you eavesdropping on us? That's bad manners. I like Samuel. I like him a lot. And I might even marry him."

Liam took a few steps closer and slid into the chair opposite her desk. "Willow, you can't be serious. He's old and stodgy. No one else's wanted to marry him and that's why he's still single. Don't you get that?"

"You're single too. Perhaps he's like a precious jewel that just needs polishing, like a diamond, and that's why no one's recognized his true value."

"You can spin it any way you want, but have you ever heard of trying to make a silk purse out of a sow's ear?"

Willow frowned at him. "That's a bit rude. He's your cousin." She pulled a sandwich out of her bag.

"Exactly, and that's why I can say those things, because I know him really well. Better than you will ever know him."

She unwrapped her sandwich and then looked up at him. "Are you going to sit there and stare at me while I eat?"

He grumbled and walked away.

When Willow was finished for the day, she went to Valerie's home. Valerie was one of her mother's good friends, and Aunt Nancy's close friend, too—she might know if her mother was sick. If she knew and had been asked to keep it quiet, Willow might be able to see it in her face. If Valerie knew nothing, Willow wouldn't know where to turn. She couldn't ask her parents outright, because if they wanted her to know, they would've told her already.

When she got to the house, she saw that Valerie already had a visitor. One look at the beautiful black horse with its one white sock told her it was Ed Bontrager who was visiting. They'd been seen together more and more since Valerie's husband had died a couple of years ago. Ed had been a widower for quite some time. They weren't officially a couple and they could be just good friends, but she'd been told the pair had dated when they were young. Willow knocked on the door, and an instant later it was opened. Ed was just putting on his hat and making his way out the door.

"Hello, Willow."

"Hello, Mr. Bontrager."

He turned around. "Goodbye, Valerie."

Willow could tell by the soft tone of his voice when he said Valerie's name that the man was smitten, for sure and for certain.

"Goodbye, Ed," Valerie said with a similarly affectionate tone. She then turned her attention to Willow. "Come in. What brings you to visit me today?" She looked around. "Are you by yourself?"

"*Jah*. I'm just on my way home from work."

"You've got a job?"

"It's a one-week trial for a job at the Hostetlers' lumberyard."

"That sounds like a good position. I hope you can secure it."

"Me too. I like working there. I just hope I'm doing a good job. Tomorrow is the last day of my trial and I'll find out if they're keeping me. Say a prayer for me?"

"I will."

When they had sat down in the living room, Willow blurted out, "Is there something wrong with my mother?"

"What do you mean?"

"Do you know if she's sick or anything?"

Valerie rubbed her neck. "She has looked rather pale lately, come to think of it."

"So you don't know anything for certain?"

"*Nee*."

Willow could see that Valerie genuinely knew nothing. "Why do you ask?"

"She's been sleeping a lot. And she's also got it into her head that she wants me to marry, and *Dat* keeps asking me and Violet to make sure that we help her, even though we always help her with the chores anyway. And I saw a black car driving away from the *haus* one day, and she said it was someone from the doctor's office because she left something there after a check-up. She never has check-ups."

"That does seem odd."

"I thought it looked like a doctor driving the car. Not an office lady." Willow took a deep breath and continued, "I do most of everything now that Violet is working part time. Ah, I suppose that if I get the job I won't be able to do very much to help her. What if she's really sick, like dying?"

"Have you asked her?"

"I can't. If they haven't told us, then they don't want us to know. I figured that that's why *Mamm* wants me to get married; so I can have a child before she dies. And she'll know Violet and I will be married and she can die knowing we're both going to be okay."

"I haven't heard of anything, but I'll see what I can find out. Now you've got me concerned. She certainly hasn't been herself lately."

Willow was worried when she saw the faraway look in Valerie's eyes.

Valerie looked back at her. "I'm sure there's nothing to worry about, Willow."

"I hope you're right. Do you think you'll be able to find out?"

"I'll try."

"*Denke*, Valerie. I'll have to get on home so I can take over cooking the dinner. I think Violet went to work today." Willow stood up.

Valerie pushed herself to her feet, and said, "I'll be sure to let you know as soon as I hear anything. Don't worry yourself too much. We'll get to the bottom of it."

"*Denke*, Valerie." Willow gave Valerie a hug and

then headed out to her buggy. She untied the reins and patted the chestnut horse on his neck. "Good boy, Rusty. We'll be home soon."

The next afternoon when she was about ready to go home, Mr. Hostetler walked into the office. "Willow, I'm glad I caught you before you left."

"*Jah*, Mr. Hostetler?" She knew what was coming. He'd either let her go or he'd give her a permanent job.

"How have you liked working here?"

Her heart thumped against her chest. She desperately wanted the job. "I've loved it."

"Would you like to stay?"

"Do you mean it?"

He smiled and nodded.

"*Denke.*" She wanted to fling her arms around him and kiss his ruddy cheeks, but instead she put out her hand and he shook it.

"We're happy to have you as a member of the team."

"I'll do a good job for you."

"You already have been. You're a quick learner, just as you promised. I'll see you tomorrow morning."

"Bye." Willow headed to her waiting buggy, feeling like she was walking on air. Then she remembered she had to stop by Valerie's house to find out about her mother. The worry over her mother overshadowed her good news.

If Valerie hadn't managed to find out anything, she didn't know what her next move should be.

When she arrived at Valerie's house, she secured her horse and walked over, poking her head through the open doorway. "Valerie!"

"Come in, Willow."

She walked in to see Valerie sitting on the couch and she hurried over and sat down next to her. "Were you able to find anything out?"

Valerie shook her head. "Not a thing. I visited two of your *mudder's* closest friends and laid a few hints, but neither of them seemed to know anything. I also visited Nancy and asked her outright and she didn't know a thing."

Willow's shoulders drooped. "If she knew something, she probably would've told you."

"Nancy seemed worried, but I told her I was asking on your behalf. That way she wouldn't think we both thought independently that your mother was ill."

"*Denke.* That was a good idea."

Valerie said, "I don't know how else to find anything out."

"We might have to wait until she says something to someone."

"Perhaps. Would you like a cup of hot tea before you go home?" Valerie asked.

"*Nee, denke.* I don't feel like anything. And I need to get home to help with dinner."

"Willow, is there a possibility that you might be wrong about this whole thing?"

"I guess anything's possible. I hope like anything that I'm wrong."

Valerie slowly nodded. "Me too."

Willow walked into her home and found Violet and their mother in the living room sewing Violet's wedding dress.

"Guess what?" Willow said.

They both looked up.

"What is it?" Violet asked.

"Mr. Hostetler is happy with me and gave me the job permanently."

Violet jumped up and hugged Willow. "That's *wunderbaar.*"

"Very good," her mother said, smiling, while Violet sat back down. "I'm glad you're happy."

"I am." Willow could smell the dinner cooking. "Something smells nice."

"It'll be ready soon. It's just leftovers."

"When are you finishing my dress?"

"It's hanging up in your room."

"Really? You've finished it already?"

Violet put her sewing to one side. "I'll show you."

The girls ran upstairs and Willow saw the long-sleeved dark-blue dress hanging in her doorway.

"Try it on."

"Okay." Willow pulled the dress on and felt it was a little big and baggy but didn't want to say so. "It's lovely. How does it look?"

"A little on the large side, but once the cape and apron go over the top you won't notice."

Willow nodded, not too happy. She felt she was a little on the heavy side and didn't need a big dress and extra layers on top. It wasn't her special day, though; it was going to be Violet's, so she kept quiet.

Chapter Nine

Violet's Wedding Day

Over the past several days, Willow had been out a few times with Samuel but they weren't officially dating. She had also spent more time at work with Liam and knew him better too. Today being Violet's wedding day, Willow knew that both men would be vying for her attention. Each man had different qualities that she liked. Samuel was quiet and attentive while Liam was vibrant and exciting. Liam was handsome and he knew it, which made him a little cocky, in Willow's opinion. Samuel was handsome, too, in his own way, but seemed more comfortable in his skin.

Willow had been too excited to sleep because Violet was getting married in the morning. She waited until daylight and ran into her sister's room and jumped under the covers with her.

"You're getting married today, Violet. You'll be Mrs. Beiler in a few hours."

Violet slowly opened her eyes. "Is it morning already?"

"*Jah.* I couldn't sleep."

"Neither could I." Violet sat up and stretched her arms above her head. "I'll remember today for the rest of my life."

"Me too. I'm so happy for you."

"I hope everything goes well. Do you think it's funny how we don't have any visitors staying at the *haus*?" Violet asked.

"*Jah.* I thought that, but I didn't want to say anything."

"Nancy, Valerie, and even the Hostetlers have people staying at their places. I'd say *Dat's* arranged that so *Mamm* doesn't get overworked. I wonder when we'll find out what's going on with *Mamm*."

"Today. I'm going to go through their room today and see if I can find a clue," Willow said.

"Do you think you should?"

"I don't want to, but I can't figure out another way to find out what's going on."

"Let me know."

"*Jah*, of course I will."

"I'm so excited for today."

"Me too," Willow said as she pulled one of her sister's pillows closer. "It's going to be strange without you in the *haus*."

"I won't be that far away."

"Be sure to visit a lot, Mrs. Beiler."

Violet giggled. "That sounds strange, as though I should be so much older. And of course I'll visit a lot. Who else would I visit? You're my closest friend."

"I'm sorry I didn't like Nathan at first."

"Don't worry about it," Violet said.

"You knew that you liked him right away, didn't you?"

"I liked him, *jah*, but I didn't know I was going to fall in love with him. I felt sorry for the way everybody was treating him. Like he was an outsider."

Willow screwed up her face. "He *was* an outsider back then. He only came back because his *mudder* died."

"I suppose that's true."

"But that's all in the past. He's one of us now."

"And that's just as well or I wouldn't be marrying him," Violet said.

"What's the time?"

"We should get up soon. The wagon will be coming with the benches soon and we should have breakfast before that."

The wedding was taking place at their house, and all the furniture would be moved out and replaced with long benches. An annex outside the kitchen was set up for the overflow, to provide for the hundreds of meals that would be prepared. There was never an exact number of guests at an Amish wedding. Invitations were sent out to family and friends, and it was always advertised in the Amish newspapers; normally hundreds of people showed up.

The girls headed down to have breakfast and found their mother in the kitchen wiping her eyes.

"What's wrong, *Mamm*?" Violet asked her.

She shook her head. "You'll be married and gone from the *haus*. You were my little girl; you were once so tiny you were the length of my wrist to my elbow. That's how small you were and now look at you. You're all grown up and you're leaving me."

Violet sniffed and hugged her mother. "You're not losing me. I'll still be here. And now you'll have Nathan as a son."

As Willow listened, she wondered if her mother really meant that it was *herself* who was leaving all of them. Then Willow got an idea. If her mother was sick, then surely she would be taking medication. That's what she had to look for when she went through her parents' room. With hundreds of wedding guests to distract her parents, it would be an ideal time for her to sneak into their bedroom to see if she could find anything—medication, paperwork, or something else to tell her what was going on with her mother. After the wedding ceremony and while everyone was eating would be the very best time to do just that.

"I'll still be in the house, *Mamm*," Willow said.

"I know." And that was all her mother said.

A couple of hours later, Willow and Violet got ready in their bedrooms. As soon as Willow had dressed, she went to Violet's room.

"People are arriving," Willow said, looking out the window. "There's Liam and the Hostetler family. Liam looks handsome."

"Not as handsome as Nathan will look," Violet said with a giggle.

"Here he is now."

Violet raced to the window and looked at Nathan, seeing him for the first time in the suit her mother and she had made for him. "He looks good."

"Jah," Willow agreed.

They looked out the window, watching the rest of the guests as they arrived.

"And here comes Samuel with his parents," Violet said.

Willow watched Samuel as he got out of the buggy. Now that she knew him better he seemed more handsome, and he certainly looked nice in his dark suit and crisp white shirt.

Fifteen minutes later, their mother walked into the room.

"Everyone's waiting on you, Violet. Willow, you come down with me, and then Violet can walk down the stairs last."

Willow and her mother hugged Violet and then headed down the stairs. All eyes were on them as they walked down the stairs and then they walked past an excited Nathan who was waiting at the bottom of the stairs for his bride.

They watched as Violet walked down the stairs and took Nathan's hand. Together they walked to the front of the living room where the bishop stood waiting for them. Two hymns were sung and then the bishop said some words about marriage and what it meant. He likened it to Christ and His Church. Willow had never really listened to what the bishop said at weddings, but this time she did.

Then they were pronounced married.

Willow looked at her mother to see her wiping a tear from the corner of her eye. She patted her mother on her shoulder to comfort her while she looked at all of her cousins who were there with their spouses. It seemed everyone was a part of a couple.

Before Willow realized what was happening, everyone was filing out of the house. It was time for the men to exchange the long benches for tables. Due to the cold, the tables had to be set up indoors rather than in the yard like Willow's mother had hoped.

Looking around, Willow caught Samuel's eye and he walked over.

At Wedding...his eyes drinking her in. She'd
felt that...as if...they had spent
her eyes met with...in the room ...ned

Chapter Ten

While Willow was talking to Samuel after the wedding ceremony, Liam deliberately stood between them and talked about something entirely different. He was being totally obnoxious.

Being an attendant at the wedding, along with her twin cousins, Lily and Daisy, Willow sat at the main wedding table. She was thankful for that, otherwise, she most likely would've had Liam on one side of her and Samuel on the other. At first, it had been flattering having two men giving her attention—now it irritated her.

Halfway through the meal, Willow managed to slip away and she headed into the house just like she had planned. Before she went up to search her parents' bedroom, she looked out the window to see that her mother and father were still eating. She ran up the stairs, taking them two at a time, and once she was in their bedroom, she closed the door behind her. The dresser was the first thing she looked through. There was nothing there.

Then she looked in her father's bureau in the cor-

ner. When she pulled out one of the drawers, her eyes
fastened on something that she had never seen before.
It was a bottle of pills. She squinted at the small print,
and going by the long name knew it had to be medication. Willow had no idea what condition the pills were
for, but she tried to commit the long name to memory
before she put them back where they'd been. Before she
left, she searched the whole room looking for something
else. She found a repeat prescription and nothing else.

There was only one person she could tell and that
was Valerie. She couldn't say anything to Violet, not
on her wedding day. And she couldn't say anything to
Nancy because Nancy could very well say something
to *Mamm*. Willow walked out of the house and headed
to Valerie. She tapped Valerie on her shoulder, leaned
down, and whispered, "Can I see you for a moment?"

Valerie looked up into her face. "What's the matter?"

"I need to have a private word with you."

Valerie walked away with Willow and when they
were around the side of the house, Willow began, "I
found some tablets in *Mamm* and *Dat's* bedroom and
they said…they said…" She frowned. "Oh, *nee*, I've
forgotten the name."

"And are they your *mudder's* tablets?"

"*Jah*, I found them in her room."

"If you could remember, I'd probably know what
they are."

Willow looked around the corner, and seeing her
mother and father still eating, she grabbed Valerie by
the arm. "We can go in the back door and go up the
stairs and I'll show you."

"*Nee*, I can't go into their room. Bring the bottle
down to me."

"Okay. Stay here."

"I will, but be quick."

Willow grabbed the bottle and took it down to show Valerie.

"That's for stomach problems, I'm sure. And the label's come off at the top. Are you sure they're for your *mudder*?"

"She's the one who's sick."

"Are you certain?" Valerie asked.

Willow bit her lip. "Not really."

"It could be either of them. You better put them back."

Willow went back to the bedroom. When she pushed the door open, her father was in the room with a coat in his hands.

"Willow, you know better than to come into my room without knocking."

Willow's heart thumped hard in her chest and her throat constricted. For once, she was speechless as she stood there with her mouth gaping open and the pill bottle clutched in her hand.

He looked from her stunned face down to her hand. "What is that?"

"Nothing."

"Show me."

She lifted her hand and opened it to reveal the bottle of pills.

He stepped forward and took it out of her hand. "What are you doing with this?"

"Nothing."

Frowning at her, he asked, "Were you looking to see if you could find medication? Are you taking drugs?"

"*Nee*, I just didn't know what they were."

"If you want to take drugs, you can't stay in this *haus*."

"I don't."

He shook the pill bottle in her face. "You were try-ing to get high on drugs. I'll talk with your *mudder* and we'll come up with a suitable punishment tomor-row." He shook his head. "This isn't how we raised you. You've been acting odd ever since you started work at the lumberyard."

"I can explain."

"Go downstairs and don't ruin your *schweschder's* wedding. We'll speak again tomorrow."

They left and rejoined the wedding party.

"Where were you?" Violet asked when she sat down next to her.

"I just needed a moment."

"For what?"

"There's too much noise here. I just needed a quiet moment."

"When are things ever too noisy for you?"

Willow stared at her sister. "Okay, if you must know, I've come back from looking in *Mamm* and *Dat's* room. *Mamm's* not dying. I found a bottle of pills and they're only for stomach problems. And it could even be *Dat's*. It's not a dangerous thing." She didn't tell her sister what had just happened with her father or that would ruin the wedding. Violet would try to stand up for her and there would be a big fuss.

"Oh, that's such a relief." Violet hugged Willow. "Why didn't you tell me right away?"

"I didn't want to distract you from your wedding."

"I've been so worried."

"Now we don't have to worry about anything," Wil-low said.

"Are you sure?"

"Positive. I even asked Valerie and she said the pills weren't for anything serious."

"That's good; she's not dying. Now I can really enjoy my wedding."

Willow sat through a tense breakfast the morning after the wedding. Violet was now married and living with Nathan at their own house, so Willow was on her own. Her father had said that he and her mother would talk to her after breakfast, and get right down to what was going on. Willow knew it wouldn't be good.

"After you wash the dishes, you can join your *mudder* and me in the living room."

"Jah, Dat." Willow hurried with the dishes, trying to get it all over as soon as possible.

"Are you ready yet, Willow?" her father called out after only a few minutes.

"I'm just about to put the last of the dishes away." Willow walked out to see her parents both sitting on one couch so she sat on the opposite one.

"Why were you in our room, Willow?"

"I don't know." Willow looked down at the rug on the floor.

"Your *vadder* said he saw you with a bottle of pills in your hand. Were you looking for drugs? We've heard about young people wanting to get high by taking pills or sniffing things. Don't think we don't know about all that, because we do."

Willow had been looking for drugs, or rather medication, but she couldn't answer yes to that question. She was looking for drugs to see if her mother was ill, not looking for drugs to take for herself. "Why can't you just trust me?" Willow thought they should trust her. Why should she have to explain herself?

Her father chimed in, "Because you have shown that you are untrustworthy, and a gossip."

It was an awful feeling that both of her parents thought so lowly of her. She wanted to get away from them. They were suffocating her. "Why do you both say I gossip all the time? I don't." Then she remembered she told Valerie about her fears concerning her mother's illness. Was that gossiping, if she was only doing it out of concern for her mother?

"Sometimes I don't think I know you anymore." Her mother shook her head.

Willow opened her mouth in shock.

Her father added, "Everything would've been fine if you had agreed to marry Samuel. He had no objection against it."

Her mother nodded. "*Jah.* You were getting on fine with Samuel when he was here last Sunday."

"That was a couple of Sundays ago."

"You shouldn't correct your *mudder*," her father said.

Willow took a deep breath. This wasn't going well.

"And why did you have the pill bottle in your hand?" her father asked.

"I found it in your bureau."

"What were you doing going through our things, Willow?" her mother asked.

"I can't tell you."

"You will tell us, Willow, and you'll tell us the truth." Her father frowned at her.

Her mother turned to her father. "I think she should go to her room until she decides to tell us the truth."

"Good idea. Go to your room and think about what you've done. And when you decide to tell us the truth, you can come out."

Willow sat there pouting at her parents. It was so unfair.

"Are you really on drugs, Willow?" her mother asked with lines deepening in her forehead.

"Of course not!"

"I'll tell the Hostetlers you can no longer work at the lumberyard," her father said.

Willow bounded to her feet. "*Nee!* That's my job!"

"You had to learn that behavior from somewhere. And your *mudder* and I noticed a distinct change in your personality since you started working there."

"*Nee.* They've just given me a permanent job. They like me. I'm good at what I do and everyone there treats me like an adult." Were they trying to ruin her life?

"If you have nothing more to say, you can go to your room now," her father said angrily. "I'm leaving now to visit Mr. Hostetler and tell him you can't work for him anymore."

Willow stood up and flounced up the stairs, closing her bedroom door behind her. She felt like slamming it, but knew she'd get into more trouble. Pulling a chair up to the window, she looked over the fields. It was a beautiful morning. The birds were chirping, the winter sun was shining, and there was a brisk wind moving the branches of the trees across the driveway.

She had to get away from her parents. She'd run away. There was no way she could live with people who didn't trust her. How could her father be so cruel after she'd worked hard in that job?

Chapter Eleven

Suddenly Willow thought of Valerie. She'd understand. *Surely Valerie will allow me to stay with her, at least for a little while.*

Valerie only lived a few miles away.

That night, after having spent the day alone in her room, she left a note in her room telling her parents she could no longer stay there if they didn't trust her. She fled into the cold night toward Valerie's home, hoping she'd be allowed to stay there for a few nights.

On her way, the chilly night air nipped at Willow's skin, so she pulled her coat higher over her neck. Did it really matter if she did not marry Samuel? She wondered why it mattered so much to her parents. In her heart, she knew that she would rather marry for love or not get married at all. How could her parents think she'd have anything to do with drugs? They treated her like a child.

Two hours later, after walking briskly across the countryside and through deserted roads, Willow came to Valerie's *haus*. She knocked on the door, hoping that it wasn't too late for visitors since the place was in darkness.

A flood of light escaped under the front door. The door opened slowly and Willow saw Valerie's silhouette against the bright light in the hallway behind her.

"Willow." Valerie looked her up and down. "Come in." She pulled on Willow's arm.

"Hello."

They hugged each other.

"I was hoping I could stay with you for just a little time."

"Of course. Stay as long as you want. What's happened? Is everything all right?"

"Everyone is okay. But everything is not. I had a dreadful fight with *Mamm* and *Dat*. At the wedding, *Dat* caught me putting the bottle of pills back in their room and now he thinks I was looking for drugs to get high on."

"Oh, Willow. That's dreadful."

"That's not the worst of it. *Dat* told Mr. Hostetler this morning that I wasn't allowed to work for him anymore. And Mr. Hostetler had just given me the job permanently. And now, through no fault of my own, I've let Mr. Hostetler down."

As Willow sobbed, Valerie rubbed her arm. "I'll help you sort things out tomorrow. We'll tell your *vadder* why you were looking for medication. I'll tell him you were only concerned about your *mudder* and bringing the bottle for me to look at."

Willow shook her head. "That would only get you into trouble. Anyway, I don't want to go back there if they don't trust me."

"It's late. You must be cold. I'll fix you some tea and cookies."

She followed Valerie to the kitchen.

Valerie filled the jug up with water and switched on the gas. "While the jug's boiling, I'll make up the bed in the spare room."

"I'll help."

Valerie's *haus* was small but pleasant and homey. There were three bedrooms and an inside bathroom. After Willow helped Valerie make the bed with fresh linen, the two of them sat down at the dining room table. Willow filled her mouth with some warm tea and swallowed slowly. It had been a cold walk to Valerie's *haus* and the tea warmed her.

"They're trying to make me marry Samuel Troyer. What do you think of that?"

"That's awful. So what do you plan on doing?"

"I don't know. I like Samuel, but there's been too much pressure. Maybe if there was no pressure things would've been different between us, but now, I don't know." Willow wanted to cry; maybe she was tired and needed some sleep. "They don't trust me and it seems they just want to get rid of me. They think I'm immature, and now they think I'm untrustworthy."

Valerie sighed. "And they think by marrying Samuel, you'll straighten yourself out?"

"*Jah.* I guess that's what they think." Valerie was married once; she was older, too, so she must know a thing or two. "You believe in love, don't you, Valerie?"

"Of course I do, and *Gott* helps me get through my days now that my husband is no longer with me."

Valerie's husband had died suddenly a couple of years ago and his death was surrounded by rumors.

Willow looked around the modern kitchen. "Your *haus* is lovely, Valerie."

"*Denke*. It's quite small, but it's just me here, so it's all I need. More tea?"

Willow looked into her empty cup. "*Nee*. I'm sorry to wake you so late."

"Nonsense. My home is your home."

Willow smiled and was grateful that she'd had somewhere to run away to.

After they said goodnight to each other, Willow closed the bedroom door. In the full-length mirror behind the door, she stared at herself. Her father had never allowed a mirror in the house, saying it led to vanity. She pulled off her prayer *kapp* and dress, trying to work out how her father could be so mean as to take away her job. Perhaps she should go on *rumspringa;* she couldn't stay at Valerie's forever, and neither did she want to move in with Violet because she was a newlywed.

Once she turned off the lamp, she slid between the covers of the bed, closed her eyes, and prayed.

Dear Gott, please help me. I don't know what to do. All I know is that I just couldn't stay at home. I hope you're not mad with me. Guide me along the way in which you would have me go. Amen.

Willow closed her eyes more tightly and hoped that *Gott* did not want her to go home and work things out with her parents. It seemed no use. No matter what she said, they took things the wrong way. They always treated her as the bad daughter, when she'd had to cover for Violet more than once when she was meeting Nathan in secret. Violet wasn't the "good daughter," not by far. So why did her parents think that she was the one to watch? It didn't make sense. Willow cried into her pillow and fell asleep exhausted.

Chapter Twelve

The morning sun beaming through the window warmed Willow's closed eyelids. Willow jumped out of bed, pulled her dress back on, and went looking for Valerie.

"You slept a long time," Valerie said as she poured some cereal into a bowl.

"Did I? I don't usually sleep late."

"It's nine o'clock. Sit down."

Willow sat at the table. "Oh, that is late for me."

"I've got to be out of here in fifteen minutes. I'm helping at a fundraiser. What will you do?"

Willow stretched her arms above her head. "Since *Dat* told the Hostetlers I couldn't work there anymore, I'll have to look for another job. I'm so embarrassed. He might have told them I was on drugs or something."

"Oh, I hope not."

"Do you know where I should go to find a job?"

"What sort of job are you looking for?"

She breathed out heavily. "I'll do anything."

"I know a friend who works at the cafeteria at the

hospital, and they're often looking for workers. I can ask her if you'd like."

Willow felt a spark of hope. "*Jah* please. That would be great."

"I know they had a job advertised last week, but I don't know if the position's filled or not. It was likely only for a job washing dishes or something not very exciting."

"I don't mind what it is. Anything is a start. I'll work my way up."

"All right. Help yourself to anything you need here, and I'll be home at six." Valerie picked up a bunch of keys and took one off. "Here's a key to the front door."

Willow held the key tightly in the palm of her hand. "I don't know what I'd have done without being able to come here. I hope it won't cause a problem between you and my parents."

"Leave that to me. I will have to tell them you're here, though."

Willow nodded, knowing that Valerie would never go behind her parents' backs about anything.

Valerie smiled, and took a last spoonful of cereal. When she finished chewing, she said, "I'll bring dinner home with me. Do you like pizza?"

"I love it."

"I'll see you tonight."

"*Denke* again, Valerie."

Moments later, Willow looked out the window and watched Valerie drive away in her buggy.

After a breakfast of toast and cereal, Willow decided to occupy her day working in the garden in front of Valerie's *haus*.

She pulled on a large apron, and a pair of heavy gardening gloves.

As she began pulling out some weeds, her thoughts turned to home. She did not want to upset her parents at all, but neither did she want to marry anyone they chose without her input. The whole situation was one in which no one would be happy.

Willow was startled by a buggy. When it drew closer, she saw that it was Liam.

She walked over and when he stopped, she asked, "What are you doing out this way?"

He jumped down. "Willow, what's going on? Your *vadder* said you could no longer work for us."

Willow looked down at the ground, and mumbled, "I had a falling out with him."

"Your *vadder*?"

"Jah."

"He can't say where you can and can't work."

"I don't want to cause any trouble at home. It's best if I don't work there if he says I can't."

"And you're staying with Valerie?"

"Jah, how did you know?"

"I passed her on the way when I was heading to your place to see how you were."

"That was nice of you."

"I care about you, Willow. Now would be a perfect time for you to run away with me."

Willow giggled and it felt good to laugh again. *"Nee."*

"Well, why don't I come back at lunchtime and take you somewhere and feed you?"

"Denke, that would be nice."

"I'll leave you to your weeding." He shook his head.

"I don't know why you're bothering. The whole place will be covered by snow soon."

Willow looked at the garden and then looked back at Liam. "What time will you be back?"

"One."

"Okay. I'll be ready."

He jumped back in his buggy and drove away.

Willow hurried back into the *haus* and looked in the mirror in her bedroom to make sure she'd looked okay. Her cheeks appeared flushed and her hair was poking out of her prayer *kapp* and could've been more tidy. She went back to finish her gardening, figuring she had to do something to pass the time.

After a stint in the garden, Willow went inside to shower and make herself look decent. Once she'd showered, she dressed in one of Valerie's dresses and brushed out her long brown hair. Valerie had said she could use anything she wished, and Willow hoped that meant clothes. After all, she only had the clothes she'd arrived in last night. Once she'd braided her hair, she fastened it to her head and placed on her *kapp*.

An hour later, Liam knocked on the door. The familiar butterflies flittered in Willow's tummy.

Liam walked through the door quickly, closing it behind him.

"We'd better keep the door open," Willow said, not thinking it proper that a single girl and boy should be alone in a *haus* together.

As soon as she'd opened the door, Liam grabbed her hand, laughing, and kicked the door shut with his foot. "Come on, Willow. We both want the same thing." He walked toward her while he undid the buttons of his shirt.

Willow backed away from him. "Liam, what are you doing? Are you a fool? Stop! I thought we would have lunch and that's all. You've got the wrong idea, Liam." She stood her ground and spoke as firmly as she could. "Please go."

Liam ignored her and lunged at her, reaching with both hands.

Willow screamed as loudly as she could.

At that moment, the front door was flung open and Samuel hurled himself through it. He looked at the two of them and pulled Liam outside the *haus*, grabbing him by his shirt. Once they were both on the front lawn, they stared at each other. Willow wondered whether they might fight.

"Get out of here, Liam Hostetler. And stay away from Willow."

Samuel towered over Liam. Liam stared up at him and said, "She likes me, cousin, not you."

"*Nee*, she doesn't like you, not that way." Samuel spoke as if he was sure of himself.

After a few seconds, Liam shook his head and walked back to his buggy.

Once Liam drove away, Samuel turned toward Willow. "Are yóu okay? Did he hurt you?"

"*Jah*, I'm okay. What are you doing here? I'm so thankful you came just now. How did you know to come here?"

"I've come to fetch you."

"How did you know I was here?" She glanced around his tall frame to see if she could see his horse and buggy since she certainly had not heard it arrive.

"Your folks thought you'd be here."

She missed her parents already, even though it had

not even been twenty-four hours. How they must be worrying. "*Denke* for rescuing me."

"That's what friends are for, isn't it?"

As she looked up into his handsome face, she finally had the feelings in her tummy that she had longed for. She was pleased that he knew that she would not have been appreciative of Liam's clumsy advances.

"What was he doing here?"

"He stopped by to see if I was okay. And then he said he was going to take me for a bite to eat because he knew I was upset. My *vadder* told the Hostetlers I wasn't coming back to work."

"Why did you run away, Willow?"

"It's a long story. My parents don't trust me; that's the main thing. And they were trying to force me to marry you, but that's not the main reason."

He lowered his head. "I know what you mean. It's horrid and embarrassing to be pushed onto someone else."

She raised her eyebrows. "You feel that too?"

He laughed.

"It certainly is funny when you think about it," Willow said.

"I've always liked you, Willow, and that's what I told my *mudder* once. I didn't know she'd go behind my back to your parents and make such a fuss. I never wanted you to be put under pressure."

"It wasn't you putting me under pressure. It wasn't you, it was my parents."

"I'm sorry anyway."

Maybe the two of them were a match. But their parents could not have been right, could they? "We used to talk, but then you became quiet," Willow said.

"I was embarrassed at what you might think of me, but I am glad we've gotten to know each other better lately. Why don't we both tell our parents that we will make our own choices?" He put out his large hand toward her. "Come back with me and we'll sit down and talk to your parents, okay, Willow?"

Willow shook her head. "Sit down. There's more to this."

They sat down and Willow told him about the incident with the pill bottle.

Samuel laughed. "I'm sorry, I shouldn't laugh. Couldn't you explain that to your *vadder*? And all those things you just told me don't add up to your *mudder* dying."

"I could've explained to him, but he should trust me. Shouldn't he?"

"I think parents get fearful. That's all. Come with me and we'll explain everything. You can't let misunderstandings ruin the relationship you have with your parents."

Willow pouted and folded her arms. "I'm angry with them."

"I know you are, and you have reason to be."

"They made me lose my job and they have embarrassed me."

"You need to forgive people. Put yourself in their position, and then you'll know they were trying to protect you."

"That's a funny way to protect me."

"We can't judge. They might have been fearful, and doing what they did out of fear. Fear of losing you. Why don't we go and sort this whole thing out?"

"Can I think about it?" Willow asked.

"*Jah.*"

"*Dat* won't be home until tonight anyway."

"Why don't I come back later this afternoon?" Samuel suggested.

"I'd like that."

Samuel rubbed his neck. "As long as Liam won't be back."

"I think you've scared him off good and proper."

"I hope so. Keep the door bolted."

"Don't worry. I will."

Chapter Thirteen

Nerida was so upset she hurried to her sister's house. She'd just gotten one daughter married and now the other had disappeared.

Without knocking, Nerida burst into the house. "Nancy, where are you?"

"In the kitchen."

Nerida walked into the kitchen and saw Nancy sitting down drinking a cup of tea.

Nancy's eyes grew wide and she jumped to her feet. "What's wrong? You look dreadful."

"Willow has run away from home."

Nancy gasped. "Why? She was just at the wedding yesterday."

Nerida said in a low voice. "Have your guests left?"

"*Jah*, first thing this morning."

Nerida pulled out a chair and sat down.

"Calm down," Nancy said. "I'll make you a cup of tea and then you can tell me what's upset you."

Once Nerida had a cup of tea in front of her, she took a quick sip, and then continued, "Willow has run away."

"Run away from home?"

"*Jah*, John thinks she is doing drugs."

"That doesn't sound like Willow."

"At the wedding, John caught her in our room and she had a bottle of pills in her hand."

"What pills?" Nancy asked.

"Just pills I take to settle my stomach."

Nancy frowned at her sister. "You didn't tell me there was something wrong with your stomach."

"It's just heartburn. If there was something serious wrong with me I would've told you. Anyway, John said he thought she was on drugs and was trying to get high. That's what young people do, you know."

"I think John has drastically jumped to conclusions. Willow was worried that you were sick and possibly even dying. She was around here a couple of weeks ago asking me questions about your health. She was worried about you. I think that's the connection with the pills. She was trying to find out what was wrong with you. That sounds reasonable to me."

"She was worried about me?"

"*Jah*. She thinks that you were trying to force her to marry Samuel so both your daughters would be happily married before you died."

Nerida shook her head. "Where would she get such a crazy notion from?"

"She did mention a couple of other things that either you or John said which made her think you were ill, and you were sleeping in the afternoon almost every day."

"Well sometimes I'm tired and sometimes I just feel like getting away by myself and I tell the girls I'm having a rest."

Nancy giggled. "I can relate to that."

"So you don't think Willow is on drugs?"

"Of course not! I've never heard of anything so ridiculous."

Nerida relaxed into the chair. "That's good. Now I have to find her."

"She's most likely gone to a friend's house. Don't worry, I'm sure she'll be back."

Placing her fingers over her mouth, Nerida said, "Oh dear."

"What is it?"

"John went to the lumber yard and told them that Willow could no longer work there."

"Why would he do that? She loved that job."

"He thought that's where she was associating with bad people who told her about drugs."

Nancy shook her head. "Poor Willow."

"I think we have treated her unfairly," Nerida said.

"I have to agree with you."

"We think she's a little immature for her age and we could see her getting into trouble and that's why John and I thought if she married early that would force her to grow up."

"I don't see Willow as being an immature girl at all. She's always seemed very sensible to me."

"I feel like I have failed as a parent." Nerida wiped the tears as they flowed out of her eyes.

"You're a wonderful parent," said Nancy.

"Not as good as you. You've done everything perfectly and all your *kinner* have made perfect marriages."

"And so will Willow. You just have to give her a bit of space and let her finish growing up by herself."

"I don't like the way she runs around and has to know everybody's business."

"She's outgoing."

"John and I think she should keep to herself more."

"She's got her own personality, and she likes to be around other people more so than you and John do, and there's nothing wrong with that. It would be a boring world if we were all the same."

"John said he had an aunt who was a gossiper and she didn't come to a good end. No one liked her in the end."

"If Willow is gossiping like you suspect, she'll have to learn those lessons for herself. But I think you two are wrong about that."

"That makes sense. Oh, I do hope she's all right."

"She'll be fine."

Nerida stood up. "I should go home. She might be home now and nobody will be there."

"Okay. I'll stop by later today if you'd like?"

"I'd like that very much."

Valerie came home a few hours later with pizzas, and Willow told Valerie everything that had happened.

"That's dreadful. I never thought Liam would do such a thing."

Willow swallowed her mouthful of pizza. "Well, he did."

"It was just as well Samuel came along when he did."

"I know. *Gott* sent him just then. Samuel wants me to go back with him tonight to talk to my parents."

"I think that would be a very good idea. You need to sort things out with them. And it will probably help if Samuel is there with you, since he's part of the issue. And part of the solution, it seems. I told your parents today that you were with me."

"What did they say?"

"They were relieved to know where you were."

Willow slumped further into her chair. "I didn't think they would care."

"Of course they care, Willow."

"They don't seem to trust me for some reason. And I've never given them any reason not to trust me."

"Things will work out, you'll see."

"I hope so."

"These pizzas are good."

"They sure are, aren't they?" Willow agreed.

"*Denke* for weeding the garden. It was getting a little bit ahead of me. The plants don't grow in this weather but the weeds seem to grow no matter what the weather."

"I had to do something here all day."

When they both heard a buggy, Valerie said, "That might be Samuel now."

Willow jumped up and looked out the window. "That's him. Oh, Valerie, I borrowed your dress. I hope you don't mind."

Valerie giggled. "I don't mind. I've got plenty. The color suits you. It brings out your eyes."

"I hope things go well tonight and if they don't, would you mind if I come back to stay here tonight?"

"*Jah.* You're always welcome here."

"I'll let you know what happens." Willow leaned down and gave Valerie a hug before she hurried outside to Samuel, who was just turning the buggy around.

"How are you feeling now?" he asked as she climbed up next to him.

"I'm still a bit shaken over what happened with Liam. I never thought he would do such a thing."

"Me either. I'm going to have a talk to him about it later."

"Don't get into a fight with him."

"I won't, but he can't go around doing things like that. I hope he'll listen to sense so I don't have to go to his *vadder*."

"Have you figured out what we are going to say to my parents?"

"*Nee*, I haven't. We'll just say what's on our minds and on our hearts. You will have to tell your parents the true reason that you had the pills in your hands at the wedding."

Willow nodded. "I suppose I should."

"Because if your *mudder* is ill, the last thing she needs is you having a disagreement with her."

"That's very true. That makes me feel bad."

"We'll make sure that we put things right tonight, Willow. And we will tell them that we don't want anyone to force us to be together. I think they already know that and have given up on it, but we'll tell them that anyway. I've already told my parents."

Willow nodded and was pleased that she had such a good friend as Samuel.

Half an hour later, Willow and Samuel sat before her parents. Willow could see how pleased her mother was that she was home, whereas her father didn't look very happy at all.

"Willow has something to tell you both about the pill bottle," Samuel said.

"We're listening," Willow's father said.

It was hard for Willow to begin; she didn't know where to start and it took her a couple of moments to get her thoughts arranged in her head. "I don't know if it's true or not, but Violet and I thought that you were very sick, *Mamm*."

"Me?"

Willow nodded. "There was the man driving away from the house in the black car. He looked like a doctor."

"He was."

Mamm and *Dat* exchanged glances.

"What's wrong?" Willow asked.

"We'll talk about this later, Willow. This is not the right time."

Willow guessed whatever it was they had to tell her, they didn't want to say it in front of Samuel.

"Are you okay?" Willow asked.

"*Jah*, I'm fine."

Willow felt tears falling and couldn't stop them. "Violet and I thought you were dying and wouldn't last very long and that's why you were so steadfast on me marrying Samuel. Then there was the doctor coming away from the house and *Dat* kept saying to help you more and then you've been having those afternoon sleeps."

Willow sobbed and Samuel sat there with his hands in his lap, looking empathetic but calm while Willow's mother rushed to sit next to her and put her arm around her shoulder.

"Oh, you poor girl! There's nothing serious wrong with me! I'm perfectly fine."

Willow hugged her mother.

Samuel added, "Willow told me that she didn't want to ask you if you were terminally ill, so she got the idea to have a look in your room during the wedding and that's when she found the pill bottle."

"I took the bottle out of the room and asked someone who said it was for stomach problems. I was putting the pills back when you found me, *Dat*. I'm not a drug taker. I wouldn't think of it and I wouldn't even know what to do with drugs."

Her father lowered his head. "I'm so sorry, Willow. I had no idea you were going through so much torment about your *mudder*. You should've said something."

Samuel said, "Willow didn't want to say anything because she said if you wanted her to know her mother was ill, you would've told her."

"That's right," Willow managed to say between sobs.

"Your *vadder* and I feel dreadful, Willow. We're so sorry we misjudged you. Will you accept our apology?"

Willow wiped the tears from her face. "I forgive you. As long as you trust me from now on."

"We will, and I'm sorry about your job, Willow," her father said.

Willow knew she wouldn't want to go back anywhere near where Liam was, so she was no longer too worried about losing her job. "That's okay, *Dat*. I'll get another one. I'm sure Mr. Hostetler will give me a good reference."

"And there's another matter that Willow and I would like to raise while we're here."

"What's that?" John asked.

"Willow and I don't want to be forced into marrying each other, or anyone else. I think it's only normal and natural that Willow and I find our own people to marry." He chuckled. "I haven't said that very well, but I think you know what I mean."

John nodded. "And I think that's fair enough."

"Shall we move to the kitchen and have a cup of hot tea?" Nerida said.

"That's a good idea. It's a lot brighter and happier in the kitchen," John said.

After the tea, Willow walked Samuel to the front door.

"*Denke* for coming with me tonight, Samuel. It made so much difference. They listen to you."

"I'm glad I could help. Bye, Willow."

He walked away and she was a little disappointed that he didn't ask to see her again. Was this the end of it, after all they'd been through? She felt her heart sinking.

He paused at the bottom of the porch stairs, turned around, and then hurried back to her.

"Willow, would tomorrow night be too soon to see you again?"

Willow couldn't help but smile as her heart soared, even though she was trying to keep her face straight. "That would be lovely."

"Really? Even though we told your parents what we just told them?" he said with his wicked, funny smile.

"We only told them that we didn't want them to force us together. So what we do after that is our business."

"That's what I hoped you were going to say. Can I pick you up at seven?"

Willow nodded and closed the door, smiling all the while.

Chapter Fourteen

Willow woke the next morning deeply pleased that she was back at home and had mended fences with her parents. She leaped out of bed and changed into her clothes, hoping to talk with her father before he left for work. When she walked into the kitchen, however, she found only her mother there.

"How are you this morning?" her mother asked.

"Really good. Has *Dat* gone?"

"He left about an hour ago."

Willow sat down at the kitchen table. "I wanted to see him before he left."

"Your *vadder* and I feel really bad about what happened. We should have trusted you like you said."

"It doesn't matter now that we've all learned something from it."

"We have. Would you like a cup of coffee?"

"Yes, please. What did you and *Dat* have for breakfast?"

"We had pancakes, and there's still plenty of batter left if you would like some."

"I'll make some for myself after I have coffee, thanks, *Mamm*."

Her mother placed a mug of coffee in front of her and then sat down. "What are you going to do today?"

"I want to wash Valerie's dress and take it back to her and thank her for being so kind to me."

"You can't put the machine on for just one dress. Wait till it's washing day. I'm sure Valerie's got plenty of other dresses."

"That's true. I saw when I borrowed this one that she has a lot. But I'd still like to stop by her place anyway."

"You can do that. We've always got a spare buggy now that Violet is using her husband's buggy." Willow's mother giggled. "I think that's the first time I've said 'Violet' and 'husband' together in a sentence."

"*Jah*, it does sound a little weird, doesn't it? I suppose we'll get used to it. I'm going out with Samuel tonight. He's picking me up at seven."

"Samuel?"

"*Jah*, he and I have grown quite close."

"I could tell by the way he was looking at you last night that he really likes you. There is a softness in his eyes every time he looks at you."

"Really?"

"I wouldn't say it if I didn't know it was true."

Things were turning out so well that happiness welled up inside Willow.

The day flew by, and all of a sudden Willow found herself waiting for Samuel. She felt like a young girl waiting to open Christmas presents. Maybe her parents did know something. At least she knew she had her parents' approval of him, which is more than what Violet had with Nathan at the beginning of their relationship.

"He's here," Willow said when she saw the buggy lights coming toward the house in the darkness. She ran and hugged her father and then her mother. "I'm glad you're not dying, *Mamm*."

Her mother giggled. "Me too."

"I won't be late." She grabbed her shawl, hurried down the front steps of the house, and met the buggy when it drew level.

"Hi, Willow."

"Hello," she said as she climbed into the buggy next to him. "Where are we going?"

"Have you eaten?"

"Just a little because I didn't know if we'd be eating or not."

"I have a surprise for you."

"What?"

He laughed. "You'll have to wait, and then you'll find out when we get there."

"I like surprises, but I want to know now."

"Just wait. Tell me how things are with your folks now."

"So good. Everyone's a lot happier and I'm so relieved *Mamm's* not really sick like Violet and I thought she was."

"*Jah*, that would be a relief. I talked to Liam, and he apologized on his own initiative, and he said he's going to apologize to you too."

"*Ach nee*. I don't even want to face him again."

"You'll have to. He wants to say he's sorry. You have to allow him that much. He'll never do it again."

"Okay. Now, are you going to tell me where we're headed, or not?"

"Not."

"Oh, come on."

He laughed. "Wait and see."

She slumped back into the seat. A few minutes later, she said, "This is the way to Nathan's house. And Violet's, now. Is that where we're going?"

"*Jah.* That's the surprise. I saw them today and they invited us there."

"Really? That's *wunderbaar.* We'll be the first couple they've had there for dinner. Wait till I tell *Mamm* and *Dat.*"

"Was that a good surprise?"

"*Jah*, the best."

He chuckled.

Samuel and Willow walked to the door.

"I didn't bring anything. If I had known we were coming here, I would've brought something. I would've brought some dessert or something."

"I'm sure Violet will forgive you. She knew I planned to keep it a surprise."

"I hope so. This is a big thing for her, having the first people over for dinner."

Samuel chuckled as he knocked on the door. It was only days after Violet and Nathan's wedding and they hadn't gone on a honeymoon or to visit relatives like most newlyweds did. Nathan was building a house on some land he had. The new house would be bigger than the one they were in now, and it had more land surrounding it.

Together Violet and Nathan opened the door.

"He surprised me," Willow said.

Violet laughed. "He said he was going to. Surprise!" Violet said hello to Samuel and then pulled Willow inside the house.

While Willow helped Violet make gravy in the kitchen, Willow told her everything that had happened in the last few days. She described the big fight she'd had with their parents, how she'd run away to Valerie's, and how they'd made up, and she also told her about Liam. And she finished by saying, "And that's why I don't mind that I don't work at the lumberyard anymore. Also, I will have to look for another job. I liked working."

"Wow, that's a lot to happen in a few short days. You've hardly drawn a breath."

"I know. Enough drama! So…did you enjoy your wedding?"

"I did. Everything seems to be happening so fast."

"Are we the first people you've had over for dinner?"

"Jah."

"That's good. That's how it should be, having your sister over for dinner. And it smells like you're having chicken."

"We're having chicken, baked vegetables, mashed potatoes, and sauerkraut. All your favorite food."

Willow smiled. *"Denke.* That's so nice of you."

"We saw Samuel just as we were heading into the markets and we invited him to dinner because he said he was taking you out. Nathan said why not come to our place for dinner, and Samuel said he'd surprise you with it." Violet whispered while the men were in the other room, "Hope you don't mind me inviting him. I know you're getting along well with him, but normally I check with you first about things like that."

"I didn't mind at all. It was a *wunderbaar* surprise to come here."

"Good. I like him."

"And I'm liking him more and more," Willow said.

The two couples sat down and had a meal at the dining table, which was in one corner of the living room.

Chapter Fifteen

It was the following week, and Violet had been invited back home to spend Thursday afternoon with Willow and their mother. It was a day off for Violet, and Willow was still looking for a new job. The sisters arrived at the *haus* together, and when they walked in, they were surprised to see their father there as well.

"Is everything okay, *Mamm*?" Suddenly Willow recalled that her mother never did tell her what was wrong with her, why she had to take that stomach medication. Perhaps it truly was something serious.

"Your *mudder* and I have something to tell you," their father said.

When they had sat on the couch, one to either side of their mother, their father sat down on the other couch opposite the three women. Willow looked nervously back and forth between their parents.

Mamm said, "We've kept something from you these past months because we wanted to be sure before we told you anything."

"Are you ill?" Violet asked.

Mamm smiled gently. "No, girls, don't be worried. I have been *feeling* a little ill, but that's because I'm pregnant."

Willow's mouth opened wide and she looked at Violet.

"Nee!" Violet said, wide-eyed. "Is it true?"

Mamm nodded and Violet jumped up and then leaned down to share a hug with her mother, while *Dat* cautioned her to be careful and not hug too hard.

"I'm so happy, *Mamm*, but I'm just shocked. I can't believe it. I thought you were too old." Violet sat back down.

"I thought so, too. And I wasn't dying like you two feared, I'm just having a *boppli*."

"This is exciting," Willow said, "but it's also a little weird. When Violet has her first, his or her aunt or *onkel* will be just a tiny bit older."

"What does it matter?" *Dat* said. "That's not so unusual in our community. It happens in families with lots of children, where a mother and her eldest daughter or daughter-in-law might have babies at the same time."

Willow looked over to see that her father was all but grinning. "You look so happy, *Dat*."

"*Gott* has blessed us with one more child. It's the best gift that a man can have."

"I was worried you girls mightn't be happy about this news," said *Mamm*.

"Of course we are," Willow said, while Violet agreed with a nod. "I just can't wait. So that really was a doctor I saw going away from the house?"

"*Jah*, he was delivering the news in person. I'd had some tests run, because I wasn't feeling myself, and he didn't want to make me wait for answers. It was the last—the very last—thing that I expected. I don't even remember him telling me that he was running that test."

Willow wiped away a tear and hugged her mother. It was the best news ever.

It was six weeks into dating Samuel regularly that Willow wanted desperately for him to ask her to marry him. She was visiting Violet to see how she could hurry the process along.

"Violet, what can I do to make him ask me to marry him?"

"Well, *this* is a turnaround."

"I always liked him. Well, once we got a chance to talk to each other alone."

"So why were you making such a fuss? If you had just gone along with *Mamm* and *Dat*, you could've already been married to him."

Willow shook her head. "Don't remind me of all that."

Violet giggled.

"You like being married, don't you?"

"I like being married to Nathan. I don't know if I'd like being married to anyone else."

"Well, that's what I meant. So you like being married to him?"

Violet's face beamed. "I do. It's lovely to have someone special who's so concerned and so loving towards me. Are you sure you're ready?"

"I am. And every day I go out with him, I hope that today will be the day that he proposes. What if he never does?"

"I'm sure he will, sooner or later, but he probably doesn't want to rush things with you."

"What do you mean?"

"Is your memory that short? Remember all the fuss that happened at the beginning?"

Willow slumped down further in her chair at the kitchen table.

Violet continued, "Have you given him any hints?"

"I didn't know I had to. What kind of hints?"

Violet rubbed her nose. "Something to let him know that you would say yes if he asked you. Have you ever talked of marriage with him, or ever talked about the future?"

"Not really. Is that a bad sign?"

"Not necessarily. He could be waiting until he knows that you would definitely say yes. It's a hard thing for a man to ask a woman to marry him. He would feel dreadful if you said no, and that might be the end of your relationship, and he definitely wouldn't want that."

Willow slowly nodded. "I see what you mean. I never thought all this would be so hard."

"Are you definitely convinced he's the one for you?"

"*Jah.* I would never be interested in any other man. He's just so good and he's so kind and I love everything about his face. And he can be so funny or so serious, and I never know which to expect."

Violet giggled at her. "When are you seeing him again?"

"Tonight. He's collecting me, and then we're going over to his parents' place for dinner."

"Again?"

"We've only been over there twice."

"When he's driving you home, just drop some hints."

"I'm no good at these things. What should I say?"

Violet licked her lips. "Let's see now... I can't really think of anything."

Willow leaned forward. "Think hard, Violet. I can't ask him to marry me. Can I?"

"Some women do, and you could if you want to, but he might not like it if you do."

Willow groaned. "If I have to ask him, I have to ask him. I can't go on like this for much longer. I want to marry him and be alone with him and have our own place just like you've got your own place. Look at how happy you are now."

Violet nodded. "I am happy."

"Just help me out, will you? What can I say when he drives me home tonight that would be a hint?"

"You could say something like, 'What do you think of marriage?'"

Willow shook her head. "That's a bit dumb."

"You think of something then. That's the best I can come up with."

Sighing, Willow said, "I'll give it some thought."

"You really don't have to. I'm sure he'll ask you soon. He's in love with you, too."

"Do you think so?" Willow's face lit up.

"Of course. Everyone knows that."

"I still can't believe *Mamm's* having a *boppli*. I won't be the youngest anymore. You'll still be the oldest and my place will be lost."

"It won't be lost, it'll just be moved up."

Willow giggled. "That sounds better. Have you gotten over the shock of it yet?"

Violet shook her head. "I'm still getting used to it. It was a shock, but a good one."

Throughout the dinner that night at the Troyers', Willow kept thinking of what she should say to Samuel when he drove her home. She wanted to let him know she would definitely say yes if he asked her to marry him. Having to say something to him was making her tummy squirm.

"More dessert, Willow?" Mrs. Troyer asked her.

"No, *denke*."

"No?" Mr. Troyer asked, looking quite surprised.

The last two times she'd had dinner at their house, she'd had two desserts. She would've had a third helping if she'd been at home, but she didn't want the Troyers to think that she was greedy.

"I've had sufficient, and it was all so good."

When Willow stepped into Samuel's buggy to go home, Willow decided that it was unromantic for her to give him any kind of hint about marriage. She would let him take his own time, and she hoped it would be wonderful and romantic when he finally proposed. Surely he knew how she felt about him. They spent most of their free time together and got along great. If he didn't know how she felt about him, there would have to be something wrong with him.

As they clip-clopped down the moonlit road, in the darkness, Samuel glanced over at her. "You've been very quiet tonight, Willow."

"Have I?"

He glanced over at her again. "You have. Unusually so."

"Dinner was lovely. Your *mamm's* such a *gut* cook. And now, I'm just enjoying the lovely night. I love the crisp night air this time of year and how it makes my cheeks tingle."

"Is that all?"

"*Jah*, and I'm just thinking about the job interview tomorrow as well. I really want the job."

"You're not worried about anything?"

"*Nee*, I'm not. Do I look worried?"

"You looked a bit worried through dinner. Are you happy with us—you and me?"

"*Jah*, I'm very happy with how things are going between us."

"That's a relief." He gave a nervous laugh. "I thought you might be getting sick of me or something."

"I could never get sick of you—never ever in a million years."

He laughed. "Are you positive about that?"

"I'm surer about that than I've ever been about anything."

"I can rest easy, then." A few yards further, he pulled the buggy off to the side of the road.

"What's going on?" Willow asked.

He turned to face her. "Willow, there's something I've been meaning to ask you."

She looked into his face. "What is it?"

He reached out and took hold of her hand. "If you still feel this way about me in a few years, do you think we might possibly get married? Do you think that will ever happen?"

Willow frowned. *In a few years?* She was ready to marry him now. "Why a few years?" She couldn't help

herself from asking; the words came out of her mouth
as though they had a life of their own.

"I want to wait until you're ready. I know you're
very reluctant about marriage."

Willow didn't know what to say. "I'm not reluctant
about marriage. I just didn't want to be pushed into it."

"The last thing I want to do is put pressure on you."

"*Nee*, you're not. I meant pressure from my
parents—our parents. It's not right. But I'm not reluctant about marriage."

"I'm pleased to hear it."

"Marriage is a good thing," Willow said, hoping
that was enough to nudge him in the right direction.

"When might you be ready for marriage?"

She put her other hand over his. "Samuel, what are
you asking me?"

He gulped. "Would you…would you marry me
in—"

"*Jah*, I will." She had to jump in fast because she
knew he was going to say, 'in a few years.'

A smile spread across his face. "Really?"

She nodded. "*Jah*, really."

"Do you mean… Are you saying that you'll marry
me now?"

"I'd like that."

He laughed. "That makes me happy—very happy."

He squeezed her hand a little and that made her
heart pitter-patter.

"You don't think it's too soon, or you're too young?"
he asked.

"*Nee*. I'll be eighteen real soon, and I think everything is just right. You don't mind if I work in a job,
do you?"

"*Nee*, you can do whatever you want. Most women work outside the home to bring in an extra income in these hard times, but I make enough so you don't have to. Do what makes you happy."

"Good."

"Let's turn around and tell my parents that we're getting married."

"*Nee*, then mine won't be first to know," Willow said.

He drew his eyebrows together. "Hmmm. I can see we'll have to work it out to have them all in the same place."

Willow said, "Let's all have dinner with Violet and Nathan, and we can tell everyone then."

"How far away will that be? I want everyone to know now. I want to yell it from the mountaintops."

Willow giggled. "I can talk to Violet tomorrow on the way home from the job interview. I'll ask if we can have that dinner as soon as possible."

He leaned in and said quietly, "Are you able to keep the secret for that long?"

"It won't matter if I just tell Violet, will it?"

Samuel laughed. "I knew it. I know you well already. When did you start liking me? Because you didn't like me when your parents and my parents were trying to push us together."

"It was just after that, actually, when I went to apologize to your mother, and you and I talked outside your house. That's when I first got to know you better. And what about you?"

"When did I start liking you?"

Willow nodded.

"I've always liked you, as far back as I remember

knowing who you were. I told my *mudder*, and she must've said something to your parents, and things got out of control from there."

Willow moved to rest her head against his shoulder. It made her feel good that he'd liked her for a long time.

"I'll get you home." He put one arm around her, and with the other he signaled with the reins for the horse to move back onto the road. "I don't need to get into trouble with your *vadder* for getting you home late."

Willow was pleased that she was about to embark on the new adventure of marriage. She'd be a young bride and if it was in God's will she'd be a young mother and her child could play with her new brother or sister. By that time, Violet might have a child too. In less than two years, there could be three babies in their family.

"What are you thinking about, Willow?"

"Thinking about you and what our life will be like together."

"I only hope your parents haven't changed their minds."

"*Nee*, they love you. Trust me on that one."

He chuckled as he stopped the buggy outside her house. She slid across the seat to get out and he grabbed her hand, leaned forward, and gave it a quick kiss.

She smiled at him. "Good night."

"I'm seeing the bishop tomorrow and I'll make the arrangements."

"What? Before our parents know?"

"He'll keep it quiet."

Willow giggled, pleased that he was just as anxious to marry her as she was to marry him. Everything had gone perfectly when she'd left things in God's hands.

She told herself that was something she'd need to do more often.

"Good night, Samuel."

He blew her a kiss before he turned the buggy. Willow watched him leave. As she walked into the house, she tried to put it out of her mind that their parents really had known best.

Chapter Sixteen

Willow's Wedding

Weddings weren't Valerie Miller's favorite functions. In fact, all the weddings she'd been to in the past years had filled her with sorrow, even though she did her best to be happy for the couples getting married. Her unhappiness with weddings began when the man she loved married another woman. This wasn't a case of sour grapes; the man in question had professed his love to her and just weeks later he married someone else.

That was something from which Valerie had never recovered. Trying to hide her pain, she gave in to Dirk Miller and finally agreed to marry him. The cure for her ailment, which was marrying Dirk, only made matters worse when Dirk accused her of still being in love with Ed. It was against God's rules and, of course, against the *Ordnung* to love a married man, and she fought against it the best she could, turning her attention to making her marriage a happy one. She'd realized as far back as on the day of her wedding that the marriage had been a mistake, but by then it was too late.

How could her marriage be happy when Dirk realized she still was harboring feelings for another man? Dirk was always raising Ed Bontrager's name and throwing it in her face. It couldn't have been easy for Dirk, but as much as Valerie pushed her feelings for Ed aside, her marriage wasn't happy.

Valerie looked over at her young friends sitting at the main table of the wedding feast. Willow, the daughter of her good friend, had just married Samuel. Always being one to offer her help in the kitchen, Valerie was now on a designated break and would soon be back in the kitchen, when it was time to start serving the next course.

Ed, now widowed for some years, moved from the table where he'd been and sat down beside her. "Don't you just love weddings?" he asked, smiling at her.

Nee! I don't! she thought. The thought sent a shiver along her spine. She pushed her dreadful wedding day from her mind.

Giving him a quick smile while pushing a forkful of food into her mouth, she thought how best to answer his question without sounding bitter. How did he expect her to answer? It was a funny question coming from him, seeing what he'd done to her. They would've had a wonderful marriage, hadn't he known that? If only he'd chosen her.

Now that they were both widowed, they'd spent a great deal of time with one another. Lately, Ed had hinted of marriage, but Valerie's wounds ran deep. How could she forgive the man if he'd never apologized for not informing her he'd fallen in love with another?

"They look happy," Valerie said, looking across at

the young couple and skillfully avoiding answering his question directly.

"*Jah*, they do."

She ate some more.

"We could be just as happy."

She gave him a sideways glance. It was another of his hints that they should marry. If he ever asked her outright, she would tell him what stood in their way. "Could we?"

"Well, don't you think so?"

"Depends."

"Some things make sense, that's all."

Had his first wife received a proper and direct proposal of marriage? "Some things seem to make sense, but then you find out they don't make sense at all."

"What's holding you back from being happy, Valerie?"

She turned and looked into his blue-green eyes. *He'd* stopped her from being happy the moment he married another woman. "I am happy. I'm always happy. I wasn't too pleased about selling off my land, but I got to keep my *haus*, and the chicken *haus*, and enough land for a large vegetable garden, so I can't complain about that. I would say I'm generally cheerful all the time." She tried not to dwell on how her late husband had left her in financial ruin due to his inability to manage their farm properly.

"Good to hear. Good to hear," Ed said, seemingly oblivious to the overdue explanation he owed Valerie.

She looked down at her food—roast turkey and her favorite baked vegetables, with cabbage and apple salad. All she wanted to know from him was why. It had been more painful to learn about his wedding to Rita from someone else. Maybe if he'd been man enough to tell her he'd fallen in love with another woman, her pain wouldn't have been so great. To hear nothing from him had made her feel worthless.

They never talked about what happened back then, but they needed to. That's what he should've been talking about, rather than dropping hints about marriage.

Valerie again glanced up at young Willow. She was so young and didn't realize how blessed she was to be marrying the man of her choice. Why hadn't things worked out for Valerie? Normally she buried her feelings deep inside, not wanting to be a bitter and twisted old woman who begrudged others their happiness because she'd had none of her own.

A childless widow was what she was. That was not the life she'd thought she'd have, back when she'd been a young girl looking forward. She'd assumed she'd have a happy home with a man she loved, and raise a brood of children. Looking around her she saw nearly everyone else had that happiness. If only she hadn't still loved Ed so much. It hadn't been easy to block her heart against this man for so long.

Swallowing hard, she turned to Ed. Maybe he had loved two women, or had he not loved her at all? Even if he'd loved her, he'd loved Rita a shade more because she was the one he'd chosen to marry.

"What is it?" he asked softly.

Shaking her head, she looked back at her plate and politely pushed her fork into a piece of turkey. "Nothing."

"Something's been bothering you for a while. Won't you tell me what it is?"

One of them had to start the conversation and she

was done waiting for it to be him. "Well, the thing is, I've always been wondering—"

"Mind if we join you two?"

They looked up to see Nerida and Nancy holding a plate of food each.

"Of course we don't mind, sit down," Ed said.

Nancy's eyes twinkled. "We didn't know if you two were having a private conversation or if anyone could join in."

"We weren't talking about anything important, were we, Ed?" Valerie asked.

"I guess not."

Valerie was relieved she hadn't mentioned anything, because he should be the one to tell her what happened back then.

Valerie was glad that Nancy and Nerida had sat down with them. The two sisters were always so vibrant, and since Dirk's death, they'd become her good friends.

Even though Nerida's youngest daughter, Willow, had just gotten married, Nerida had recently received the surprising news that she was about to become a mother again. Now her family was starting to get used to the idea. It had been a shock to both Willow and Violet because, they said, their future children would be very close in age to their new sibling, who would be an aunt or uncle to their babies.

It wasn't long before Ed excused himself. "I can see I'm outnumbered. I'll go find some men to talk to."

Nerida and Nancy giggled at what he said, and then he turned around and gave Valerie a big smile before he left.

"Things are progressing there, I see." Nancy gave Valerie a little wink.

"We've always been good friends."

Nerida leaned forward. "And now becoming a little more than friends?"

"Just you worry about knitting booties for your new *boppli*."

"That's quite some months away. I need to keep myself occupied with something in the meantime."

"Don't look at me." Valerie finished the last of her food.

Nancy leaned across the table and spoke in a low voice. "I've been quiet about this for some time, Valerie, but you and Ed together…it just makes sense."

Valerie raised her eyebrows at Nancy saying something so similar to what Ed had just said. Then she fiddled with the strings of her prayer *kapp*, twisting them through her fingers. "There's more to these things than you know. Anyway, just because you've got the last of your girls married off, don't go thinking you can turn your attention to me, trying to get me married." Valerie laughed as though she didn't care about getting married. She wanted to marry Ed, but only if he acknowledged how he'd hurt her, and gave her a sincere apology. Then they'd be able to move forward. She gestured toward the crowd. "I'm sure there are plenty of young girls here who would love your help in finding husbands, Nancy."

"*Jah*, and I'll work my way through them. *Gott* has given me the gift of matching people. I just want to see you happy, too, Valerie," Nancy said.

"I am happy. I'm happy every day of my life."

"But with a man, your life would be so much better." Nerida dabbed at her mouth with a napkin when she finished swallowing a mouthful. "It's nice to have someone to share your life with, don't you think?" She stared at Valerie, waiting for her to respond.

Sharing her life with Dirk really hadn't been good, but she would never admit to that. "There are good things about being on your own, and there are good things about being married. At this time in my life I choose to be alone, and surely that's my choice to make. There's nothing wrong with being alone."

Nancy drew back as though she'd been struck. "If that's what you want, Valerie. I would never try to push you into something you didn't want. You and Ed are always together. I thought for certain you'd marry and I thought you two would be married before now."

"*Jah*, we both expected it, didn't we, Nancy?"

Nancy nodded. *"Jah."*

"We want you to be as happy as we are," Nerida stated flatly.

Valerie tried to throw them off the track. "Well, I am. I'm not sure about Ed. Maybe he doesn't want to marry again."

Nancy leaned forward. "What?"

"Nothing. Look at Willow," Valerie said, just to change the conversation. "I've never seen her look so happy. She's simply glowing."

They turned around and looked at Willow.

"She certainly is," Nerida said when she turned back around.

"And you're glowing too, Nerida. Your skin is simply radiant."

That made Nerida happy. A definite hint of a smile appeared around the corners of her mouth.

"Nerida and John's news was a big surprise to everybody," Nancy said of Nerida's late-in-life pregnancy.

As the women chatted about the new baby, Valerie occasionally looked around for Ed. She couldn't deny there was still a bond between them even though a good part of her wished there wasn't.

After a while, Valerie stood up, excused herself, and headed back to the kitchen.

With her hands in sudsy water and scrubbing dishes, she figured all thoughts of "happy ever after" would be the last things on her mind.

"What do you think is wrong with her?" Nancy asked Nerida once Valerie had left them.

"Haven't you noticed she's always like this at weddings?"

"*Nee.*"

"Well, I've noticed. She didn't have a happy marriage with Dirk."

"I know that," Nancy said. "Do you think that's why she and Ed have never gotten married?"

Nerida rubbed her belly. "I'm guessing it started way before that. Something happened in the past. Do you remember she and Ed dated before Ed got married to Rita?"

"*Jah*, I thought that's how things were."

"What happened?" Nerida asked.

"I don't know." Seeing Nerida staring in disbelief, she said, "I can't know everything about everyone."

"I thought you might have heard something from Hezekiah since he's close with the bishop and must get to hear things. I'm just saying that something must've happened. Something caused them to split up—to break up—and when they did, Ed didn't waste any time getting married."

Nancy nodded. "You're right. They had some hiccup. They must've. I wonder if it was just because they were too far away from each other with her still living in Ohio and Ed being here and spending the other part of his time in Lowville?"

"Was he in Lowville to see Rita?"

"*Nee*, his *onkel* and other *familye* are from there. As far as I know, he was working there some of the time."

Nerida said, "They had a disagreement about something. And maybe they still disagree about the same thing and that's why they're not married."

"*Jah*, you must be right. There's something they disagree about."

"Although, I can't think what that would be."

"It doesn't have to be anything that big," Nancy pointed out. "Many couples argue about things that are small."

"Do you think we should find out what it is and see what we can do about it?"

"*Jah*, of course. We must. I'm sure she'd be much happier if she was married and neither of them is getting any younger."

"We'll have to make a plan," Nerida said.

"And we can't let Valerie know what we're doing. She acted weird right now when we mentioned Ed and marriage."

"Maybe it's Ed who doesn't want to get married, like she suggested. Did you think of that?"

Nancy drummed her fingers on the table. "We'll have to find that out before we formulate a plan."

They looked around for Ed and saw him talking to John, Nerida's husband.

"Let's go and talk to him now."

Nerida shook her head. "We can't. We can't risk John finding out what we're doing. He won't approve."

"It's Valerie's birthday coming up soon if I'm not wrong."

"That's not until next month."

A smile brightened Nancy's face. "I'll have a big birthday dinner for her at my place and I'll be sure to invite Ed. And then we'll gauge how they are with each other when they're in the same room."

"It seems a long way away."

"It is, but we've got to be clever about this. We can't let anybody know what we're doing so we can't do anything out of the ordinary. And having a birthday dinner for Valerie would be something that we'd normally do."

Nerida nodded. "You're right. Okay, we'll arrange that."

"Good."

Chapter Seventeen

Just as Valerie had finished with washing her break-fast dishes, she heard a buggy making its way toward the house. A quick glance out the kitchen window showed her it was Ed Bontrager's black horse pulling the buggy. This was nothing unusual since he visited her nearly every day. Sometimes his visits would be brief and sometimes he would stay for an hour or two and they would simply talk and pass the time together as friends.

She opened the front door and waited for him. As soon as he came closer and she saw his face, she knew he was troubled about something.

"What is it, Ed?"

He took off his hat as he walked up the porch steps and then he smoothed down his gray hair. "I have something to ask you."

"*Jah*? What is it?" Had he finally come to ask her to marry him? Today might be the day when all her questions would be answered. "Do you want to sit out here on the porch, or would you like to come through to the kitchen?"

"Just here will be fine," he said, gesturing to the two porch chairs.

She moved to sit in the farthest porch chair, and he sat next to her.

"What is it, Ed? You're worrying me. You look quite disturbed about something."

He chuckled. "There's nothing wrong. I've received a letter from Rhonda."

She couldn't recall anyone called Rhonda. "Who's that?"

"Rita's *schweschder*."

He didn't seem happy. "Is she ill?"

Ed chuckled again. "*Nee*, she's quite well. She wants to come here for a few months to see if she'd like to move here to live. Her husband died a few months ago, and she's all by herself."

"Oh. She never had any *kinner*?"

"*Nee*. I was hoping you wouldn't mind if she stayed with you."

"That'll be fine. I'll be glad of the company, and it sounds like we've got a lot in common. We both lost our husbands, and we both have no *kinner*."

He leaned back. "*Denke*. That's a load off my mind. I feel better knowing she'll be staying here with you."

"When is she coming, do you know?"

"She said she'll be here as soon as she finds a place to stay. She sent a letter to the bishop, but I thought you would be the perfect person for her to stay with."

"Of course. Has she ever been here? I don't recall her visiting."

"She's been here a couple of times over the years, but only stayed a couple of days at a time. Her husband had a lingering illness, and needed constant care, so it was hard for her to get away."

"Ah, that must've been hard for her."

He nodded. "It was."

"I look forward to her staying here. I'll clean out the spare bedroom and re-wash all the linen."

"I didn't mean to put you to too much bother."

"It's no bother." Valerie laughed quietly, remembering her silly notion that he might be there to propose. "Would you like a cup of *kaffe*?"

"*Nee, denke.* I have a new apprentice starting today and I don't want him to think I'm never around the place."

"Okay."

He stood up and gave her a smile before he placed his hat back on his head.

Valerie watched Ed's buggy head back down the driveway. It was nice to have his friendship, but would they ever be more than close friends? What would it take for him to utter those words?

Later that day, on the way home from the markets, Valerie stopped by Nancy's house to tell her friend that she would soon have a visitor.

As she sat at Nancy's kitchen table after delivering the news, Nancy said, "The bishop has only just now asked Hezekiah and me if we would have Ed's *schweschder*-in-law stay here, at our *haus*. We've got all those spare bedrooms now."

"Oh, Ed mustn't have realized that Rhonda was organizing things through the bishop. Come to think of it, he did mention that she had written to the bishop."

"It's all arranged. I spoke to Rhonda myself earlier today on the telephone."

"Here I was coming to give you some news, and instead you've got the news."

Nancy laughed, and then after she'd had a mouthful of tea, she said, "It would be a bit awkward, though, don't you think?"

"What would be awkward?"

"To have her stay with you. Rhonda is Rita's *schwescher*. Don't you think it would be awkward if she stayed at your *haus*?"

"I can't see why."

"Because you and Ed used to be so close, and you're still close." Nancy shrugged. "Forget I said anything."

"I'm not sure what you mean, Nancy."

"It's like this. What if Rhonda's coming here in the hopes of marrying Ed? He's a widower and she's a widow." Nancy wiggled her eyebrows.

Valerie gasped and covered her mouth. "*Nee!* I didn't even think of that."

Nancy lifted her chin just slightly. "She lost her husband a few months ago, and she has nothing to keep her at Lowville. Why wouldn't she want to marry Ed? He's a good man, he's hard-working, and he's got a good business. Even at his age he's a catch."

Valerie remained quiet, thinking about what Nancy had said. "But don't you think that would be weird, marrying her late *schweschder's* husband?"

"It's not as though it hasn't been done before, Valerie."

Valerie slowly nodded, thinking of two marriages where someone married the sibling of their late spouse. "You're right."

Nancy put two elbows on the table and stared at Valerie. "So what are you going to do about it?"

"Nothing. What can I do about it?"

"Get a commitment from Ed before she gets here. A commitment of marriage."

Nancy could've had no idea what she'd just said. Valerie had once had a commitment of marriage, but Ed's commitment of marriage had been worthless. Even though it hadn't been a verbal commitment, he'd given broad hints that they would marry and there was talk of creating a future together and buying a *haus*.

"Well, don't you think so?" Nancy asked.

Valerie shook her head. "Commitments mean nothing."

"Well then, marry him before she gets here."

Valerie shook her head. "If Ed's so easily swayed by another woman, then he and I are not meant to be."

"Don't you have any understanding of men, Valerie Miller?"

"Of course I do—I think. What do you mean exactly?"

"Men don't know what they want most of the time. It's up to us to decide for them what they want. If you really want Ed, and you're in love with him—and I think you are—you must take steps to make it happen."

"I can't. Somewhere in my heart is the romantic notion that a man must want me and only me. If Ed doesn't feel that, then I would rather live the rest of my life alone."

"Surely not!"

"It's not so bad by myself. I enjoy my own company and the solitude. I can do what I want when I want without having to ask a man anything, and I don't have to compromise."

That got Nancy talking and Valerie watched Nancy's mouth open and close, open and close. There was no point listening to what she was saying. All Valerie knew was that if Ed chose Rhonda over her, it would be like him marrying Rita all over again. And if that happened, she would sell up and move back to Ohio where she'd lived as a girl. She still had plenty of family there, and that's where she would spend the rest of her days.

Chapter Eighteen

A week and a half later, Nerida visited Valerie and when Valerie saw her pull up at her house, she hoped Nerida had news of Rhonda, who'd arrived in the community two days ago.

Ten minutes later, Nerida suggested they both visit Nancy so they could meet Rhonda before the Sunday meeting.

"We might as well stop by," Valerie said.

"You'll do it?" Nerida stared at Valerie.

"I might as well meet her now. I'll have to sooner or later."

Nerida's eyes opened wide. "Right now?"

"Isn't that what you meant?"

"Okay, let's do it."

Valerie looked around her house at all the things she was going to do that day. There were the rugs that needed taking outside to be given a good beating. The gas light fixtures needed dusting, and then there was the washing. "I've got washing hanging on the line."

"And it will be there when you get back. I'll bring

you home again. We only need be there for an hour or two."

Valerie nodded, figuring an hour would be well and truly enough. "I'll switch off the gas and we'll have a cup of hot tea over there instead."

"Okay. I wonder what she's like."

"I thought you would've met her already."

"*Nee*, I didn't want to overwhelm her. I thought she might have too many visitors at the start. Now she should've settled in a little."

Valerie switched off the gas and left the kettle on the stove. "Have you heard anything about her? It was the first time Ed had mentioned her to me when he asked if she could stay here."

"I remember her visiting Ed and Rita many years ago. And she was here for Rita's funeral."

"What's she like?"

"She's a small woman and she looks similar to Rita."

"Makes sense, I guess," Valerie said.

When they knocked on the door, Nancy led them through to the kitchen where a small dark woman with elfin-like features sat on a chair at the table. Valerie guessed her to be around fifty. Even though her skin was smooth and wrinkle-free, the slight sagging of her neck and jowl area told the story of her age, as did the silver streaks running through the dark hair in front of her prayer *kapp*.

Rhonda immediately leaped to her feet and put her hand out. "You must be Valerie."

She was a good six inches shorter than Valerie, and Valerie couldn't help but wonder if that appealed to

Ed, who was only an inch taller than herself. Valerie smiled and extended a hand. "I'm pleased to meet you."

"Likewise," Rhonda said with a charming smile. "And you've got to be Nerida?"

"Jah."

Rhonda smiled and shook Nerida's hand, and then looked back at Valerie. "I do apologize for not staying at your place, Valerie. Ed told me you had kindly offered, but before that, the bishop found me Nancy's place to stay."

The woman was attractive and polite. She seemed friendly enough, but it didn't escape Valerie's notice that the woman had only spoken three sentences and had already mentioned Ed.

"Would you two like hot tea?" Nancy asked.

Seeing they were already in the middle of a cup of tea, Valerie thought it was only polite to join them. *"Jah,* please. That would be lovely."

"We can't stay long, I'm afraid," Nerida said to Nancy.

Once they'd sat down and Nancy was fussing around, making more hot tea, Rhonda turned her attention to Nerida. "You must be thrilled to be expecting another *boppli.* I was so excited for you when Nancy told me your news."

"It was quite unexpected. I'd gone to the doctor for an entirely different reason and it was a big shock. John is extremely happy, but it took the girls a little while to get used to the idea."

Nancy interrupted. "Nerida's girls said their *kinner,* when they have them, would likely be only a year or two younger than their aunt or *onkel.*"

"Do you have *kinner*?" Valerie asked Rhonda before she remembered that Ed had said that she didn't.

"*Nee*. Peter and I weren't blessed with any. That's why I was disappointed that Ed wouldn't move back after Rita died. I could have been a bigger part of my nephews' lives."

"I don't have any either, and my husband passed away a couple of years ago now," Valerie said.

"*Jah*, I know. Ed told me."

"And how long can you stay for?" Nerida asked Rhonda.

"I'm staying for a few weeks. I've got a vague idea in the back of my head that I might move here one day. I'll look at places to buy while I'm here, to get a feel for what's available."

"That would be *wunderbaar*," Nancy said as she placed a fresh teapot in the middle of the table.

"While I'm here, I'm going to keep myself busy. Ed's been alone for so long and he needs someone to look after him."

Valerie looked down into the empty teacup in front of her and jumped when Nancy poured hot tea into it.

"And exactly how are you going to look after him?" Nancy asked.

"For starters, I'm making him new curtains. That is if I can borrow your sewing machine, Nancy?"

"Of course you can."

"Is it a treadle machine?" Rhonda asked.

"It is."

That must've been the right answer because Rhonda looked happy about that, Valerie noticed. "What curtains are you talking about? Because I made him curtains just last year for the living room."

Rhonda giggled. "Oh, I'm so sorry. They look like they've been there for many years."

"*Nee*, they're quite new. Did Ed say he wanted them replaced?" Valerie asked.

"Not at all. I spotted them and thought that was something I'd be able to do for him. Anyway, I didn't want to make you feel bad, Valerie. It was a careless thing for me to say."

"That's okay."

"Did you make him new bedroom curtains?"

"*Nee*, I didn't."

"Well, I'll make him curtains for his bedroom, and all the bedrooms. How many bedrooms does he have in his *haus*?"

"Four, I think," Valerie said.

Holding the teacup in both of her small hands, Rhonda brought the cup to her lips and took a delicate sip. "You're a particularly good friend of Ed then, Valerie?"

"Ed and I have been good friends for many years."

"He never mentioned you in any of his letters. I only heard your name when he said you offered a place for me to stay. That was very kind of you, *denke*."

Valerie smiled and nodded politely, but remained silent, resisting the temptation to tell her that Ed had never mentioned her either.

Nerida cleared her throat. "What else do you have planned for your stay, other than looking at houses and making curtains?"

"I'd like to have another look around the area. Ed will be able to show me around when he's not working. I told him he needs to stop working so hard." Rhonda giggled. "At his age he should slow down, particularly since his boys are working in his business. Surely they can run the place—that's what I said to him."

"And what did he say about that?" Nancy asked.

"He said he likes working. It keeps his mind and body active. He said he'll keep working as long as he's able."

"That sounds like Ed," Nerida said.

"Don't get me wrong, I like men who work hard, but there comes a time when a person has to take their age into account. Ed's not as young as he thinks he is. Anyway, it's not my place to tell him what to do." After she drank some tea, she looked at Valerie. "What did your husband do?"

"He ran the farm."

"Ah, the one you had to sell?"

"*Jah.* How did you know?"

"Ed told me. At least, I think it was Ed."

"Dirk worked the farm by himself. We only had a small plot of land compared with others."

"Working the land is hard. My husband owned four successful businesses before he fell ill. We had to sell two of them, but I've still got managers in the others."

"What kind of businesses?" Nerida asked.

"Two Amish small goods stores, a bike shop, and we also had a block of storage units. We sold the storage units and the bike shop. And I might as well tell you that I'm selling the two small goods stores as well. I have a cousin looking after that for me while I'm here."

Valerie couldn't drink her tea fast enough and when she finished, she gave Nerida 'the nod.'

"*Denke* for the tea, Nancy. I've got so many things to do today."

"Me too," Valerie said. "It was nice meeting you, Rhonda, and I'll see you again at the meeting."

Nancy and Rhonda stood at the door and waved as Valerie and Nerida drove away from the house.

"Well, what do you think?" Nerida asked Valerie.

"She seems nice."

"What about what she said about the curtains?"

"I know, but she didn't know I'd made them. You can't blame someone for that. If she'd known, it might be a different story."

Nerida shook her head.

"She seemed nice," Valerie said again.

"I guess."

After breakfast the next morning, Valerie was sweeping the boards of the porch when she saw a buggy heading to the house. When it got closer, she saw it was Nancy and she was by herself. Relief washed over her.

Rhonda made her feel tense for some reason. After she had rested the broom against the house, she walked over to meet Nancy who was now tying her horse to the fence.

"What's going on? How did you get away without Rhonda?"

"She's gone into town with Nerida. And what I thought was right. She's here with one thing on her mind and that is to marry Ed."

Valerie sighed. "That was plain to see yesterday. She couldn't stop talking about him."

Nancy fixed her eyes on her. "Valerie, I think it's time you told me the whole story."

"The whole story of what?"

"Why you and Ed didn't end up marrying years ago when you were dating. I recall you lived in Ohio and Ed used to travel to see you and then you used to come here to stay with someone for weeks at a time."

Valerie's gaze fell to the dirt beneath her feet. "I'll make us a cup of tea. It's a long story."

Once they were comfortably sitting on the couch with a cup of tea in hand, Valerie began, "This feels a little strange to tell you something that I've held so close for so long. I've never shared this with another person."

Nancy's eyes widened.

"Oh, don't look like that. It's nothing secretive or spectacular. It's just a painful story of how a young girl was rejected by the man she loved."

"I'm sorry," Nancy said in a barely audible voice.

Valerie took a deep breath. "I was living in in Ohio, and Ed, as you know, was living here. I suppose that wasn't good from the start, but we visited one another often. Even though we lived so far apart, we had an understanding that we would marry. He was saving up to buy a small plot of land and we talked of building a *haus* and a life together." Valerie shook her head. "I can't even tell you if his plans were six months or two years into the future; all I knew was that we were going to be together."

"Well then, where did things go wrong?"

Valerie swallowed hard. "I knew he had family in Lowville because he used to go there often. He sent me two letters from there and then all of a sudden his letters stopped. The next thing I knew was someone told me they'd read of his wedding announcement in one of the Amish papers. I forget who it was who told me.

And that was when I learned that he was getting married. At first I thought there was another Ed Bontrager somewhere and that it couldn't possibly be my Ed."

"Did you get a letter or anything from him explaining what happened?"

"Nothing! Not a letter, not a phone call, nothing. It was two years later when I was visiting this very community that I saw him again with his new wife and she was pregnant with their first child."

Nancy shook her head. "That must've been hard."

"Dirk asked me to marry him and I said yes because I was trying to bury the pain and I'd found no other way to do it. I thought marriage and another man would take my mind off Ed, but it only made me miserable."

"I didn't think you were happy in your marriage. I just knew something was wrong."

"It was a dreadful thing to do, to marry for those reasons. Dirk deserved somebody who loved him. I know that now. My hasty decision just made two people miserable for a very long time. But it served its purpose in that it kept my mind off Ed. I saw him all the time but what we'd had together became a distant memory."

"How did it come about that he married Rita?"

Valerie looked directly into Nancy's eyes. "He has never told me, even after all this time. I guess he just found that he loved her more than me."

"And you think that's all?"

"What more can there be?" Valerie asked.

"That makes sense now. The pieces fit together. Except it seems such a hasty marriage for Ed to marry Rita and not even tell you that he was getting married."

"I guess he fell in love. And they had a happy marriage as far as I knew."

"I never heard otherwise." Nancy sat in silence while remembering Ed and Rita. They certainly had seemed to have a happy family.

"Anyway, it's all so far in the past it barely matters anymore."

"I know that's not right, Valerie. I know you're hurt and I've always wondered about it."

"Maybe it'll hurt more if I know the truth."

Nancy shook her head. "The truth sets us free. Surely you'll feel better to know than to keep wondering?"

"Maybe, but don't trouble yourself over it, Nancy. What's done is done."

Nancy nodded. "I should keep going. I've got a lot to do today."

"Okay. *Denke* for stopping by."

When Nancy got back into the buggy and drove away from Valerie's house, she wiped away a tear caused by Valerie's sad story. It was a terrible thing to love someone and then find out they were marrying someone else.

"How could you do this to her, Ed?" she asked aloud.

That was a question she needed answered. Figuring Nerida and Rhonda would be in town for some time, she headed to Ed's workshop. Ed owned a glazier business and did work for all the Amish people, and he serviced a good number of the local townsfolk.

She would ask him outright what happened and why he didn't tell Valerie he was getting married. Then a thought occurred to Nancy. There was every possibility that Valerie had misread their relationship. If she hadn't, Ed had been too cowardly to face Valerie.

Then again, should she keep out of the whole thing?

Too often, Hezekiah told her, she meddled in people's lives and he thought she should just leave things be. But what if it happened to Valerie again? Rhonda was obviously in town for the sole purpose of marrying Ed.

Since Dirk's death, Ed and Valerie had grown increasingly close and if there was any chance for Valerie to marry the man she loved, Nancy decided, then she would help things along the best she could.

When she drew closer to the glass factory and saw Ed's horse, she was glad he was there. Ed's horse was distinctive. He was black all over except for one white sock on his right front leg. Nancy secured her horse and walked into the large barn of a workshop. She caught the attention of Jacob, one of Ed's sons, and waved him over.

"Hi, Jacob. Is your *vadder* about?"

"Yeah, he's out in the back. I'll take you through to his office and then tell him you're here."

"Denke."

She followed Jacob to a small office away from the noisy factory floor. Someone was sizing glass with a cutting machine and it was making an earsplitting sound.

Jacob closed the door of the office behind him once Nancy was seated, and the sound was barely audible.

Still hoping she was doing the right thing, Nancy looked around the bare office. An old wooden desk separated the two chairs, and in one corner of the room sat a small refrigerator with a water dispenser on top.

Ed swung the door open and walked through.

"Nancy, this is a nice surprise. Do you need some glass, or are you visiting?"

"Neither. I need to discuss something with you. Do you have the time?"

"I've always got time for you, Nancy."

He sat down, appearing stiff and rigid. He was nervous about what she was about to ask, that was clear.

"I've just come from Valerie's."

"Is she all right?"

"*Ach jah.* She's quite all right, but... Oh dear, you'll think I'm being nosey. I need to ask you something, but I'm not doing it for bad reasons or to be a gossip. It's just that Valerie is a very good friend of mine and I know you two have been getting along so well. The thing is, I need to ask you a question."

"What is it?"

"You don't have to answer it if you don't want to."

"It must be a very important question if it's brought you here to see me."

"It is. I'll be blunt."

He nodded. "I find that's always best."

"I just talked to Valerie and she told me that long ago she expected that the two of you would marry." She stared at Ed and saw him shift in his seat. "Did she have things the wrong way around in her head back then?"

He moved his gaze from her and shook his head. "*Nee.* We were heading for marriage."

"Why didn't it happen?"

"Because I married Rita."

"I know that, but Valerie feels she is owed, or she was owed, some kind of explanation. You never told her you'd fallen in love with someone else. She was

shocked to hear it from somebody else." Nancy put a
hand on the wooden desk, hoping Ed would take everything she said okay and wouldn't take offence.

"Did she ask you to come here?"

"*Nee.* She only told me this because I was probing.
I know you two like one another and I just want you
both to be happy. She would never ask me to talk to
you on her behalf—never. Valerie holds her feelings
close to her heart."

Chapter Nineteen

Ed looked down at the swirling patterns of wood grain on the desk in front of him. What could he have said to Valerie? He certainly couldn't have told her the truth. The secret was not his to tell. It wouldn't have been the truth to tell her he was in love with someone else because he wasn't. He'd only ever loved Valerie, but he'd had to put her out of his mind and learn to love the woman he was married to and that's what he'd done. He grew to love Rita, and they were happy together and they raised a happy family.

"Ed?"

He looked back up at Nancy.

"Why didn't you talk to her about it?" she asked.

If Nancy was demanding an answer, how much more was Valerie wondering about the matter? "It was a long time ago. I didn't tell her and then, as the time went on, I was married and a conversation with Valerie about our previous relationship would've been wrong. You're right, though. I should've said something back then, before I married Rita."

"I don't think it's in the past for Valerie."

He'd failed the woman he loved. "I didn't realize."

"It's still something that…well, I believe it's something that she still hangs onto."

Now it made sense to Ed that Valerie was still hurt about the past, and that's why she hadn't been receptive when he mentioned their future together.

"Every woman wants to feel special, Ed," Nancy said. "Not telling her you were going to marry Rita made her feel worthless—like you didn't care enough to tell her. Didn't you owe her that, simply as a courtesy?"

Ed nodded. He knew it must've hit Valerie hard when she learned about his marriage, but at the time he hadn't been able to find the words to tell her.

"Ed."

He looked up at Nancy. *"Jah?"*

"Did you bring Rhonda here so you could marry her?"

"Absolutely not. That is the furthest thing from my mind. She's Rita's *schweschder.* Why would you ask?" He saw Nancy raise her eyebrows, and that confirmed his suspicion that Rhonda must've had marriage on her mind. He shook his head. "Is that why she's here?"

"I believe so. I don't know for certain, but I'm not often wrong on these matters. That's why I'm here. I didn't want anything to get in your way with Valerie, if that's where you both were headed."

He rubbed a hand over the stubble on his chin. He'd shaved off his beard a year ago. Amish men only grew their beards after marriage, and Ed had shaved his off to let Valerie know he was ready to marry again.

"What should I do about this, Nancy? I don't want to

hurt any more people, and I have no interest in Rhonda apart from helping her as a member of my *familye*."

"In matters like these, Ed, someone's always going to end up hurt. But they get hurt more if they don't know the truth from the beginning. All you have to do is follow your heart and be honest with everybody and let everyone know what's going on. I'm not sure why you married Rita, and it's none of my business, but I believe that Valerie is owed an apology about you not telling her yourself. Doesn't she deserve that?"

"*Jah*, she deserves…that, and a whole lot more."

"*Gut.*"

"*Denke* for coming here today and nudging me onto the right path."

Nancy giggled. "We all need a little nudge every now and again. It's a lot easier to look upon someone else's life and see what they should be doing. It's a lot harder to look at yourself."

"I know what you mean."

Nancy rose to her feet. "You're coming to Valerie's birthday dinner, I hope?"

"I am. Tuesday night?"

"*Jah.*"

"I'll be there."

Nancy arrived home to see Nerida's buggy near the barn. Not knowing if she was going out again shortly or not, Nancy secured her horse and walked into the house. There, in her kitchen, she found Rhonda and Nerida eating takeout chicken and French fries.

"I bought you some, too, Nancy. It's sitting in the oven keeping warm. Rhonda and I have been out."

"*Denke.*" Nancy got the takeout from the oven

and sat down with them. "Where did you go?" Nancy asked.

"We headed to town, to the stores."

"And then I saw a real estate office," Rhonda added. "We ended up having a look at two houses and I bought one of them."

Nancy looked up and gulped. That was the last thing she had expected. "You bought one that quickly?"

"I put an offer in and it was accepted. I'm signing the paperwork tomorrow."

"Already? So soon?"

"I sold my *haus* before I moved here, so it's all fallen nicely into place."

"I didn't know you'd sold your place. I thought you said you were looking at the community, to see if you even wanted to live here," Nancy said. That's what she'd told them.

"I've been here before and this is where I've decided I want to live. My mind was already made up."

"I see. Well, that's good then. We're very happy to have you here."

When she finished eating, Rhonda looked down. "I must wash all this grease off my hands."

Once Rhonda was out of the kitchen and inside the bathroom, Nancy leaned over toward Nerida. "How could you let this happen?"

"I couldn't help it. She kept taking me around to look in the windows of the real estate agents. And then a young man came out of an office when we were by the window and asked what we were looking for. The next thing I knew, we were in his car looking at houses."

Nancy shook her head.

"Don't get mad at me." Nerida made a face and touched her belly.

"Are you all right?"

"Just a pain."

"It looks like a pretty bad pain."

"I've had them all day."

"You should go to the doctor and have it checked out."

"Maybe you're right. If it doesn't ease up, I'll go to the doctor first thing in the morning."

Nancy shook her head. "A pregnancy at your age is a delicate thing. You can't take any chances. I'm driving you to the doctor now."

Rhonda overheard when she came back in the room. "What's wrong, Nerida?"

"I've been having pains on and off all day."

"You should've said something."

Nerida shrugged. "I thought they'd go away."

"We'll go in my buggy. Would you like to come with us, Rhonda?"

"*Nee, denke.* Since your buggy will be here, Nerida, do you mind if I borrow it?"

"Of course I don't mind. That's fine."

"I won't go far. I thought I would just pay a quick visit to Valerie."

Nancy called ahead and let the doctor know that they were coming.

"Now you've got me worried. Do you think there's a problem?"

"We'll soon find out. I hope there's nothing wrong. You could be having twins."

Nerida whipped her head around to look at her sister. "Do you think so?"

"It's possible. They say it runs in families, and since I had twins, you might, too."

"Two babies equals double the work," Nerida said.

"Double the *joy*," Nancy added with a laugh.

"That's true. John would be delighted to have twins. And they'd be playmates."

"Don't get your hopes up."

"I won't. It had crossed my mind a while ago that I might have twins, but I hadn't considered it lately."

"Anyway, have you thought of any names?"

"I've considered a lot of names, but I don't have any firm favorites yet. Do you have any suggestions?"

"Are you going to continue with my flower theme?" Nancy gave her sister a sidelong glance.

Nerida had borrowed Nancy's idea of calling her girls after flowers and the fact that she'd done that without telling Nancy first had caused a years-long rift between the pair. What Nerida should've done, Nancy thought, was asked her if she minded if she copied her flower theme.

"Maybe I'll continue with that theme. I've got Violet and Willow, so something that goes with those names would be good."

"Tell me some of the names you've thought of," Nancy said.

"I can't think of them off the top of my head."

"Think of them now. I'll be quiet a moment."

"I keep thinking I'm having a girl. I have to keep reminding myself it might be a boy."

"And you're thinking that there are no flower names for boys?"

Nerida giggled. "You're obsessed with your flower theme, aren't you? Would it worry you that much if I called my baby after a flower?"

"I would just like you to admit that you copied me like you always have since you've been born."

"Don't you realize that that's a compliment, that I copied everything you did?"

Nancy shook her head. "I didn't see it as a compliment. I saw it as an infringement—stepping across the line."

"But haven't we gotten past that? I thought we were forgiving and forgetting and moving onward."

"You having another *boppli* has brought it all to the fore."

"Would you be happy if I agreed to call my *boppli* something that doesn't resemble a flower?"

"*Ach nee.* You're not playing that trick with me." Nancy wagged a finger at Nerida.

"What are you talking about? I'm not playing any game or trick. Anyway, can't John and I call our *boppli* anything we want, or do we have to check with you?"

"I just want you to be open with me. I don't want to find out... I don't want to be the last to find out that you've called your daughter a flower name. Something like Heather, or Jasmine, or Marigold."

"*Denke.* Those are some nice names. I like the name Heather. What will I do if I have a boy? There are no flower boys' names."

"I think there are. I didn't call my sons flower names. I only thought of it when Rose came along. Otherwise, I would've called one of them Cedar. It's a strong, manly name. And then there's Basil. Or Heath."

"Those are all nice names."

"So, then, are you saying that you will give your baby a flower name, or not?"

Since there was no traffic on the road, Nancy stared at her sister while giving the horse his head, allowing him to make his own way up the road.

"I don't want to cause any trouble between us, Nancy. There's already been too much trouble and too many years that we spent not talking to each other over this silly thing."

"It wasn't silly to me."

"Of course it was silly, and still is. You don't own any names. Even if I decided to call my child Rose, it doesn't matter because you don't own that name."

"Are you considering calling your child the same name as one of my daughters?"

"Of course I wouldn't do that. That would be too confusing. That's not the point I'm trying to make."

"What point are you trying to make, Nerida?"

When Nerida pulled a face and put her hand on her stomach, Nancy felt bad about getting into a heated discussion. She urged her horse on.

"I'm sorry. Forget I ever said anything. Nothing matters. Call the *boppli* whatever you want."

Soon they were sitting in the waiting area of the doctor's clinic.

The doctor stepped out of his office and called out Nerida's name. Nancy was left alone to leaf through Hollywood gossip magazines. She picked one up and made a start but soon threw it back down on the coffee table.

It was awful of her just now to pick on her sister. It didn't matter what Nerida called her baby, or what her motivation was. Considering her sister's delicate condition, Nancy was ashamed of herself for raising the subject in the first place. She closed her eyes and prayed for forgiveness, and that the baby would come into the world healthy and safe. It wasn't long before she was interrupted by a man and his young son, who sat down close to her.

Valerie was sitting at her kitchen table peeling vegetables when she heard a buggy. As she so often did when she heard a buggy approaching, she hoped it was Ed. She hurried to the kitchen window and saw it was Nerida's buggy. If she knew Nerida at all, she was certain Nerida was stopping by to tell her something about Rhonda.

After she had wiped her hands on a towel and opened the front door ready to greet Nerida, she saw Rhonda walking toward her and no sign of Nerida.

"Hello, Rhonda. You're by yourself?"

Rhonda blinked her dark eyelashes and smiled her usual bright smile. "*Jah.* I hope you don't mind me stopping by."

"Not at all. I'm happy to see you. I was just keeping myself busy."

"Nerida had pains and Nancy took her to the doctor."

Valerie gasped. "*Nee!* What kind of pains?"

"To do with the *boppli*, I'd imagine."

Valerie felt sick to the stomach. "I hope she'll be okay."

"She looked okay. It was just a precaution. Nerida didn't think it was necessary to go, but Nancy talked her into it."

"I'm glad she did."

"Don't you think Nancy is a forceful kind of person?"

"Just as well she is. It's best to be on the safe side. I'm happy she insisted Nerida go to the doctor. Come in and I'll put the kettle on."

"*Denke.* Nerida said I could borrow her buggy while she was at the doctor and I thought it would be a perfect chance for the two of us to get to know one another better."

"Oh, that's nice. Good idea." Once they were in the kitchen, Rhonda sat while Valerie lit the gas flame and placed the kettle on top. Valerie hoped the next several minutes wouldn't be too awkward and hoped Rhonda wouldn't talk about Ed's curtains again.

"I've bought a *haus*," Rhonda announced abruptly.

Valerie's eyes flew wide open. "Around here?"

"*Jah*, I saw it today. A nice man drove me to look at two. Nerida was with me. I liked the second one so much I put an offer in."

"That was fast."

"I had to move quickly because the realtor said he was expecting another offer on it. The owners verbally accepted my offer, and I have to sign the paperwork, the contract and such, tomorrow."

"Are you having it looked at by a builder first?"

"Do you think I should?"

"*Jah*, of course."

"I don't know any."

"I'm sure Ed would know someone who could look at it for you."

"*Jah*. Or maybe Ed himself could?" Rhonda suggested.

Valerie nodded. "Maybe. You'd need to know if it needed a lot of repair work or something."

"It's fairly new."

"Still, it's best to be certain."

"You're right. I'll go to Ed's place when I leave here. Then I'll make arrangements with the realtor to have it inspected."

"Good. You do move quickly on things."

"Once I make up my mind about something, I like to move fast."

"*Jah*, I'm the same, but that's too quick for me. You only got here a couple of days ago. Is your new *haus* close by?"

"It's only fifteen minutes from here."

"That's not far."

Rhonda giggled. "I've noticed we're fairly similar, Valerie. We're both widows and we have no *kinner*."

"That's right. We'll become *gut* friends, I'm sure."

"And it seems like we're both close to Ed."

Valerie smiled. "He's a very good friend."

"You knew him before he was married, didn't you?"

"I did. Our friendship goes back quite a long way."

"I don't know what people around here know and don't know about Ed. You might be able to help me. I wouldn't like to put my foot in it and bring up things that nobody knows."

The woman was hinting she knew things about Ed that no one else did, but what could that possibly be?

"Just a minute." When the kettle whistled, Valerie got up and poured the hot water into the teapot, wondering whether this woman was a bit of a mischief-maker. When they each had a cup of tea and she'd set a plate of cookies in front of them, Valerie sat back down. "Now, what is it that you're worried about?"

"*Denke* for the tea. I was saying that I often put my foot into things. And I don't want to have Ed upset with me. He's the one who suggested I move here, after all."

"Cookie?" Valerie moved the plate of cookies closer to Rhonda.

"*Nee denke.* I don't eat between meals."

That explained how she stayed so small. Valerie couldn't imagine *not* eating between meals. "So, you know things about Ed and you think people around here won't know them? Does Ed have secrets?" Valerie forced a smile as she warmed her hands around the small teacup.

"That's what I'm trying to work out, and since you're such a good friend of his, I want to run it by you first. Does everybody know that Ed and Rita *had* to get married?"

"Why would they have had to get married?"

When Rhonda stared at her with wide eyes and raised one eyebrow slightly, Valerie caught on to what she meant.

"Ah, they *had* to get married?"

Rhonda nodded, and it upset Valerie that Rhonda would tell her such a thing. And for what purpose was she telling her?

"That's right, because they were expecting."

Chapter Twenty

Valerie was shocked that the woman in front of her was sharing that kind of news, but more than that, she was upset with Ed. He'd said he was in love with her and then for that to happen just wasn't right. Then she added up the years. "But that doesn't add up; their oldest child was born two years after they married."

"That's right, because Rita miscarried a month or two after they were married."

Valerie put a hand over her mouth. "That's so sad."

"Rita said it was *Gott's* punishment."

"Rhonda, why are you telling me all this? It happened so long ago, and if Ed didn't tell me, that meant he didn't want me to know about it. No one else needs to know that."

"That's why I wanted to ask you. If you of all people don't know, that means no one else knows, so I must keep quiet about it."

Common sense told Valerie to leave things alone, but it annoyed her so much she couldn't. "But for what purpose would you raise this with anybody else? This was years ago and it's none of anyone else's business. It's a private thing."

"*Jah*, you're absolutely right. I didn't even think of that. I'll just keep quiet about everything else."

Valerie knew she was being baited, but couldn't resist asking her next question. "There's more?"

Rhonda pushed out her lips. "I shouldn't say anything else. I will take your advice and keep quiet about things." She looked at the plate of cookies. "One cookie surely won't hurt. And if I don't have an appetite for dinner, I'll tell Nancy you fed me too many cookies."

Valerie's mind was taken up with the earth-shattering news she'd just been told. Ed Bontrager had been a perfect gentleman with her when they'd been dating all those years ago and hadn't even tried to kiss her. To find out he'd acted vastly differently with someone else was quite unbelievable. He must've known that Rita was the woman he'd marry; that was the only thing that made sense.

Valerie didn't want to let Rhonda know that she was upset. She'd put it out of her mind while Rhonda was in her house. "I do hope Nerida will be okay."

"From what I know of pregnant women, they often have pains and things like that. I'm sure she'll be perfectly fine."

"I know, but she is a little older than most women in her condition. Her doctor told her she was in a high-risk category and once she's further along, she needs to be monitored regularly."

"Don't worry. I'm sure she'll be okay."

Valerie reached for a cookie and nibbled on it, still wondering why Rhonda had told her that disturbing news. She didn't want to think poorly of the woman.

Was it just an innocent comment like she'd made out, or was Rhonda a gossip and a troublemaker? She had to give Rhonda the benefit of the doubt. "It's such a surprise, you buying a *haus* so quickly."

"Why do you say that?"

"You said you were possibly going to settle here. Moving to a whole new community is such a big decision."

"It's not that big a decision for me. I like to make up my mind about things quickly, like I just said. I already know I'll like it here and there was nothing to keep me at Lowville."

"We're always happy to have another lady in the community."

"Really?"

"*Jah*, of course. Everyone here's friendly and easy to get along with. Nancy and Nerida were so good to me when Dirk died. I tended to keep to myself when I was married, for some reason."

"I'm sorry to hear your husband died. Mine was ill for a long time. Was yours?"

Valerie was transported back to the dreadful day her husband died. They'd had words. He had accused her again of liking Ed, who'd become widowed a few years before. It had become one of the regular things that they argued about, starting shortly after Ed's wife had died. Valerie had managed to bury her feelings for Ed a long time ago. She'd done the best she could to make Dirk happy, but he'd guessed how she'd once felt about Ed and he wouldn't let it go.

Shortly after Ed's wife had died, Dirk said he felt like he was standing in the way of her and Ed being happy together. *I might as well kill myself and then you can marry him.* Those were the bitter words he'd uttered. Later that very evening, he didn't come home. That was the last time she saw him. Figuring he'd made himself a bed in the barn like he sometimes did when they'd had an argument, she checked early in the morning and he wasn't there. He was found by a farmer later that day, lying on a riverbank.

She'd never know if the drowning was a deliberate death or not. Their money worries had added pressure onto their relationship. Had he simply tried to cool off in the river, or had he carried out the threat he'd uttered? If only his last words hadn't been hateful ones when he'd walked out their door.

"Valerie?"

Valerie looked across at her visitor. "Oh, I'm sorry. What were you saying?"

"Was your husband ill before he died, or was it sudden?"

"*Nee*, he wasn't sick. It was an accident that took his life. Just an accident." Rhonda stared at her, waiting to hear more. "He drowned," Valerie finally added.

"That must have come as a dreadful shock."

Valerie nodded. "It did."

"My husband was knocking on *Gott's* door for months, nearly a year before he died. I had time to get used to the idea of him being gone and to get my mind prepared for being by myself. I had a chance to make some plans."

"I guess there's an advantage in knowing ahead of time."

"How has your life changed since your dear husband died?" Rhonda asked.

Valerie placed a cookie on her plate. "We had a farm, and I had to sell it, but you know that."

"*Jah*, you mentioned it the very first time I met you."

"There was no choice. We had debts, so I sold the land to the left of us here, but I was able to keep this *haus*. I'm grateful for that."

"I was fortunate enough that David left me with a sizable sum of money and then there was the *haus* that I've since sold. It held too many memories of David's illness. I want to remember him as the healthy man that he once was, and I'll be able to do that better from somewhere else. I need to move on from the past. Those sad days are behind me now."

"And you've moved here for a better future?"

"I have." Rhonda launched into telling Valerie more about herself.

Valerie nodded to show she was listening to her story, but she still wasn't sure if this woman was a friend or a foe. Had she told her about Ed and Rita deliberately to upset her, and to make certain that Valerie and Ed would never have a future with one another?

Rhonda giggled. "I hope you don't mind that I asked you if you knew that about Ed and Rita. I didn't know how this community was with things like that."

Valerie was shocked that Rhonda would giggle about the matter. "The same as every other community would be. No one knows that, and I dare say no one probably cares to know since it was so long ago. Ed and Rita had obviously talked to their bishop and made amends and put whatever happened behind them."

"Oh, I hope you don't think I've come here with bad intentions."

"*Nee*, I don't think that." She hoped not, anyway,

and had already decided to give Rhonda the benefit of the doubt.

"I can see by your cross face you're upset with me. *Nee, nee*, Valerie. It was as I said." She shook her head. "I always manage to say the wrong things. I've gotten into trouble in the past for my big mouth and I thought I'd run things by you to prevent that happening again. It's so much pressure to keep other people's secrets, don't you think?"

"I don't think I know anyone's secrets." Only her own and she wasn't sharing those with anyone. And certainly not with Rhonda, not after this conversation.

"I know quite a few."

"Just as well you asked about it because something like that needs to remain unsaid. Don't mention it to anyone."

She leaned forward and grasped Valerie's arm. "*Denke* for telling me, Valerie. I hope I don't slip up and accidently mention it to someone."

"That would be a terrible thing. The bishop here is firm about gossip. He says the tongue is a great destroyer."

"And he's right. *Denke*, Valerie. Now let's stop talking about it."

Rhonda seemed used to getting what she wanted and if she truly wanted to marry Ed, then that was most likely what was going to happen.

Nerida came out of the doctor's office and Nancy looked up to see her sister's face looking as white as the snowy fields on a Christmas morning.

Springing from her chair, Nancy rushed to Nerida's side. "What's wrong?"

Nerida looked around the waiting area, noticing the man and child sitting in the corner, and then whispered, "I have to have bed rest. For the next four months until the birth. Can you believe it?"

"The *boppli's* okay?"

Nerida nodded. "So far."

"That's nothing to be so upset about," Nancy said.

"That means the *boppli* could be in danger."

"Surely not if you rest."

Nerida shrugged her shoulders.

"Let's get you out of here."

Once Nerida had paid for her consultation, they headed out to the buggy.

"I'll take you straight home and then you can go to bed and I'll organize the girls to look after you."

"Willow's still away visiting and there's only Violet and John to look after me."

"I know. I was talking about my girls as well as Violet. We'll all take it in turns of looking after you and seeing to everything around the *haus*, and also see to it that John is looked after."

"*Denke*, Nancy. That makes me feel a little better."

"And you can sew while you're in bed. You don't have to be bored."

Nerida sighed. "It'll be hard not doing anything useful."

"Sewing's useful, and besides, you can have a well-earned rest because you might not get much rest after the child arrives."

"As long as the *boppli* arrives safe and healthy."

"We can make that the matter of many prayers."

"I do hate putting other people out, though," Nerida said.

"Nonsense. Everybody will be happy to look after you. Sometimes it's good for us to let others care for us."

Ed had just arrived home from work. He usually left around four and had the workers lock up when they were done for the day. He was rubbing down his horse when he saw Nerida's buggy. He squinted to see that it was Rhonda driving it. He patted his horse on the neck. "That will do you for today, boy."

He left his horse in the stable and went out to see what she wanted. She stopped the horse in the middle of the drive, stepped down, and held the horse's cheek strap. "I'm so glad you're home, Ed. I didn't know whether you'd still be at work or if you'd be home."

"I generally finish about this time of day. Can I help you with something?"

"*Jah*, I think so. I was talking to one of the girls and she said that I should have the house inspected before I sign a contract."

"What *haus*? Don't tell me you bought one here already?"

She giggled. "I forgot to tell you that first. I put in an offer on one today, and received a verbal acceptance."

He rubbed his chin. "Then you should definitely have it checked out."

"Do you know anyone who can do that?" Rhonda asked.

"I can give you the number of a friend of mine."

"*Jah*, please."

"Come into the barn. You might as well call him from here if you want."

"That would be good, and then I can call the realtor and try to make arrangements for the builder to get into the *haus*. Is that how things are done?"

"Pretty much, although it's been awhile since I bought one."

"Me too. And David used to do all these kinds of things."

He walked into the barn with Rhonda following him. He leafed through his address book and then wrote down the number of his friend on a piece of paper. "I'll give him a call if you like."

"Would you?"

"Sure. I might as well, and then I'll put you on the phone once I've told him what's going on."

After she had talked to Ed's builder friend and arranged things with the realtor, she replaced the phone's receiver and turned around, smiling widely at Ed. "*Denke*. I don't like to spend any unnecessary money, but I should, I suppose, because there might be something wrong with the *haus*."

"It's always best to check," Ed said.

"Perhaps you'd like to come and have a look at the place with me?"

"Sure. I'll try to stop by at the same time as the builder."

"Good. I'd like to know what you think of it. It's four bedrooms and it's a two level home."

"Do you need one that big?"

"I'm expecting visitors from Lowville. I hope people will visit me, anyway."

He nodded. "Of course they will."

"Well, *denke* for your help. I should be getting back to help Nancy with the evening meal."

"Any time, Rhonda."

When Rhonda headed back down the driveway in the buggy, Ed was pleased she hadn't tried to prolong her stay by asking him if he wanted her to cook him dinner.

Chapter Twenty-One

News had reached Valerie that Nerida was on bed rest, ordered by the doctor. On her way back from the markets, she stopped by the needlework store and bought Nerida a sampler and some embroidery cotton. When she approached Nerida's house, she was surprised to see Ed's horse and buggy. It was unlike Ed to visit someone during the day. She secured her horse and picked up the box of candy along with the sewing items she'd bought Nerida and then hurried to the front door.

John opened the door before she reached it.

"Is Ed here?" she asked, forgetting her manners entirely.

"*Nee.* Rhonda borrowed his buggy."

"Rhonda's here visiting Nerida?"

"*Jah*, that's right. Come in."

Valerie walked through the door. "How has she been?"

"She's doing okay. A little depressed about spending months in bed, but she knows that's what has to be done. Go on up. You know the way."

While John sat back down on the couch, Valerie

made her way upstairs. Just as she put her foot on the top step, she heard giggling coming from Nerida's room. She walked in to see Rhonda sitting on the edge of Nerida's bed.

"Hello," Valerie said.

"Valerie, this is a nice surprise. I've got so many visitors."

"I brought you candy and some sewing to keep you occupied."

Rhonda jumped off the bed and took everything from her. "Oh, what a nice little box of candy. I'll put these with the things I brought Nerida."

Valerie's eyes traveled to the nightstand where a large box of candies and several rolls of wool and various knitting needles sat. "Oh, you brought knitting. I didn't even think of that."

"Rhonda has brought me enough knitting to keep me busy for quite some time."

"I can see that."

Nerida said, "Sit down by me, Valerie, and tell me all your news."

Valerie sat down and gave a little laugh. "You've only been here for a few days. Not much has happened." She gulped and couldn't help wondering how it had come about that Rhonda had borrowed Ed's buggy. Ed was fanatical about his black horse. He was more of a pet than a work horse. Valerie looked over at Rhonda. "Anything new happening with you, Rhonda?"

"Only buying the *haus*. That's enough, isn't it?"

"*Jah*, I guess so."

Valerie was pleased to hear that was all she had to report. If something had happened between her and

Ed, she would surely have said so, since she found it hard to keep other people's secrets, much less her own.

"I thought Ed was here when I saw his horse."

"I was visiting him at work and I admired his horse and he said I could take him for a run. He knows how careful I am with horses. Ed and I share that love."

"The love of horses?" Valerie asked, hoping that was all she meant.

"*Jah.* I told Ed I was just on my way to visit Nerida and he said to take his buggy. He's a lovely horse. Have you ever driven with him?"

"I've never driven him, no." Valerie wasn't sure whether she was asking if she'd ever been in Ed's buggy or if she'd ever actually driven Ed's buggy herself. She answered as though she was asking about the latter. Valerie looked back at Nerida. "Are you doing okay? No more pains?"

"Not since I've been resting. At least it's a way of seeing more of my nieces. They've been very good about taking it in turns and coming over with their little ones."

"Good."

Nerida looked over at her sewing and knitting. "*Denke* for bringing the sewing. That will help pass the time and make me not feel so useless."

"Don't feel guilty about having a rest. It's about time you took things slower."

"I hope you'll be able to help me with the *boppli,* Valerie."

"I'd love to."

"So will I, Nerida," said Rhonda. "You can count on me. I'll be over here helping you every day."

Valerie almost felt like God had put Rhonda there

to replace her. The woman had quickly befriended all her friends and was all but throwing herself at Ed.

"Oh, Valerie, I forgot to tell you. I took your advice and had someone look at the house. Ed gave me the name of a builder friend. Anyway, there was nothing wrong with the *haus*. Just a few little things, but nothing to stop me from going ahead with the purchase. So, I thank you for your suggestion anyway."

"That's *gut* news," Valerie said.

"*Jah*. Except I had to pay the builder for doing the inspection."

Nerida said, "And now you have peace of mind, Rhonda. You wouldn't expect the man to do the inspection report for free, would you?"

"*Ach nee*, of course not. I'm glad I had it done because now I know that I was right and there was nothing wrong with it."

"Good."

"I signed the papers and I'm the owner of a *haus*."

"*Wunderbaar!* When do you move in?" Valerie asked.

"About four weeks' time. Nancy will have to put up with me until then."

Nerida said, "I'm sure she loves the company now that all her girls have gone."

"She has her *grosskinner* over there a *gut* part of the time. They can be noisy."

Valerie and Nerida laughed.

"You can always stay with me if they get too much for you."

"*Denke*, Valerie. That's very kind."

Nerida turned to Valerie. "I'm sorry I won't be able to make it for your birthday dinner. I'll be stuck right here in this bed."

"There's nothing to be sorry about. Just make sure you do everything your doctor told you."

"Most things can be fixed with herbs," Rhonda said.

Valerie and Nerida exchanged glances.

"Nettle tea is *gut* for most ailments. My *mudder* raised my *schweschder* and me to know which herbs to use, but I've forgotten most of it now. Raspberry leaf is good for women if I remember rightly." She leaned over and patted Nerida's arm. "I'll get some for you and make you a nice tea."

"That sounds nice, *denke*."

"I'm going to have Ed put in all new windows when I move into my *haus*."

"What's wrong with them?" Nerida and Valerie asked at the same time.

Rhonda laughed at them, and then said, "They rattle. They weren't put in properly. That's what the builder said. They won't have to be replaced if they can get them out and fit them better."

"Wouldn't you wait until they break or something?" Nerida asked. "It seems an awful waste and a lot of trouble to go to."

Valerie remained quiet.

"I like everything to be in nice condition and it would set my nerves on edge to listen to windows rattling in the wind."

"*Jah*, that would be annoying and it sounds like it might be dangerous, too, if they weren't put in correctly," Valerie said.

On the day of Valerie's birthday, she'd been given strict instructions to show up at Nancy's house at exactly seven in the evening.

When she arrived, she saw many buggies lining the driveway.

Willow ran out to her and Valerie barely had a chance to secure her horse before Willow wrapped her arms around her.

"You're back already?" Valerie said.

"*Jah.* We've been gone for weeks."

"Time has gone by so quickly. Are you sure it's been weeks?"

"It feels like it, visiting all those relations." She leaned in and whispered, "Don't tell anyone I said that. Now, please *don't* ask me how married life is treating me."

Valerie laughed. "I might have if you hadn't warned me not to."

"Married life is good; I'm still in love, and no, we're not expecting yet."

Valerie laughed again and put her arm around Willow's shoulder. "It's good to have you back. I've missed you. And I'm pretty sure I wasn't going to ask any of those questions. Well, maybe just one or two of them."

Willow shook her head. "Please don't, or I'll scream."

Valerie looked up at Nancy's house. "I've been given strict instructions to arrive at seven and it's seven now."

"Come on," Willow said, walking with her to the house.

No sooner had Valerie stepped a foot through the door than everyone gathered around, wishing her a happy birthday. Once she thanked the well-wishers, she glanced over at Ed, who was smiling back at her. Her smile quickly faltered when she saw Rhonda next to him.

Rhonda stepped forward and Valerie's gaze lowered to a small giftwrapped parcel in her hands. *"Nee.* I told Nancy no gifts. Didn't she tell everyone? Where is Nancy?"

Nancy called out from the other side of the room. "I've come to learn that I can't stop Rhonda from doing anything she wants."

Rhonda laughed. "It's nothing. It's just something very small. Just a token."

Rhonda was smiling so sweetly Valerie found it hard not to like the woman. *"Denke,"* Valerie said as she took the gift from Rhonda.

"You don't have to open it now. Take it home with you. Here." She took the gift from her and set it down on a table by the door. "Take it with you on your way out—when you're ready to go home."

"Okay, *denke.*"

"Dinner is ready, everyone. Take a plate and help yourselves. Sit wherever you'd like. The birthday girl is served first. Come along, Valerie."

It was odd being first when Valerie was normally doing either the serving or the cooking at events. No one had made a fuss like this over her birthday for a long time. She took a plate and filled it with the roasted chicken, bologna, sweet corn, and her favorite pickled onions.

Once she'd heaped her dinner plate, she sat down on one of the chairs and watched as a long line formed behind the table. The house was filled with happy conversation and the aroma of good food.

"Happy birthday, Valerie."

Valerie turned around to face Ed, who sat down next to her.

"Denke."

Then they were interrupted by Rhonda talking about how wonderful the food was and telling them which of the dishes she had cooked. "Oh, Ed, would you like me to fill you a plate?"

He glanced at the table. *"Nee, denke.* I'll wait until the crowd dies down and help myself then."

"You're a man and you need to be fed. I don't mind bringing you a plate."

"I'm fine, Rhonda. You worry about yourself. I'll sit and keep Valerie company for a minute."

"Okay." Rhonda walked off in the direction of the food table.

Valerie sensed that he relaxed when Rhonda was gone. "Were you surprised Rhonda moved here so quickly?" Valerie asked.

"Jah, and she didn't tell me she'd already sold her *haus* back in Lowville. I only found that out when she was buying the one here."

Not wanting to keep talking about Rhonda, Valerie changed the subject. "Are you busy at work?"

"It's getting busier all the time. I've just put on another apprentice."

"So that's two now?"

"Nee, only one. I probably mentioned him the other day."

Valerie smiled at him. *"Jah,* you did."

Their conversation was forced and not easy like it normally was.

"I see John's not here," Ed said.

When Valerie swallowed a mouthful of chicken, she said, *"Nee,* he wouldn't want to come and leave Nerida alone at home."

Ed nodded and looked around the room while his hands were fixed firmly in his lap.

"Are you okay, Ed?"

"*Jah*, I am."

"You seem nervous, or something."

He leaned in and whispered, "I'm nervous about Rhonda."

"Why's that?"

"I feel a responsibility that she settles in well."

Valerie glanced up to see Rhonda talking and laughing with people as they helped themselves to food. "She seems to be doing just fine with that."

"I've got a gift for you, Valerie. I didn't want to bring it tonight. I tried to get it to you today, but by the time I finished work, it was time to come here. I'll stop by and see you tomorrow."

"I don't need a gift, Ed."

"It's something I want you to have."

Other people came to talk to Valerie, and Ed moved away.

The next time Valerie looked around to see Ed, she wasn't surprised to see that Rhonda was talking to him. She put them both out of her mind and did her best to enjoy the dinner that Nancy and Rhonda had worked so hard to put on. When everybody had eaten the first course, Nancy produced the biggest cherry cake Valerie had ever seen.

"You remembered my favorite cake!"

"I hope it's not too far away from the one that you make."

"It looks delicious."

"We found preserved Black Forest cherries," Rhonda said, looking pleased with herself.

"Yes, they are the best ones to use."

Nancy handed Rhonda a large knife and she sliced the cake down the center.

"Now that you've done that, I'll serve everyone," Nancy said as she passed the first slice to Valerie. Valerie looked down at the cherry cake. They had remembered to make it with mock cream filled with sugar and butter and confectioners' sugar instead of the fresh cream. Most people liked fresh cream, but Valerie didn't; she liked the alternative that was richer and filled with sugar. The vanilla cake was moist and the cherries had been soaked in kirsch, a liqueur that tasted so good with the Black Forest cherries. Valerie closed her eyes and savored the flavors that worked so perfectly together.

"You look like you're enjoying that."

She opened her eyes to see Rhonda. She swallowed the mouthful. "It's *wunderbaar*, and you helped Nancy make this?"

"I did. This is the first time I've made this kind of cake, but everyone seems to be enjoying it, so I think I'll make it again."

"It's not a quick cake to make, but it's so worth it."

"I don't really like cake." Rhonda lifted her chin.

Valerie couldn't believe her ears. Who didn't like cake?"

"I can't believe you just said that. Everyone likes cake."

Rhonda giggled. "I like cookies and chocolate but not cake."

"I'll have to remember that. I'll have chocolate on hand for you the next time you stop by."

When the night was drawing to a close, Valerie tried

to help with the cleaning up, but Nancy would not hear a word of it. "Don't you dare," she said when Valerie picked up an empty plate.

"I don't mind helping."

"Not on your birthday," she said. After Nancy had looked around, she whispered to Valerie. "Now that Rhonda's busy washing up, now's your chance to talk with Ed."

Valerie smiled. "Thanks. Good idea."

When she walked out into the living room, she saw that Ed looked like he was getting ready to go home; he was standing by the door. "Are you leaving, Ed?"

"Stop."

Everyone in the house fell silent, and Ed and Valerie whipped their heads around at the sound of Rhonda's sharp voice.

Rhonda took another step toward them. "If you're leaving, Ed, you must take a piece of cake with you. And you too, Valerie." She placed a wrapped up slice of cake in Ed's hands and then said to Valerie. "Now I'll get you a piece."

"Denke," was all Valerie could say because she was still in shock at how loud such a tiny woman could yell.

Ed put his hand over his heart. "My heart nearly stopped."

"So did mine." They both laughed.

"I'll see you tomorrow, Valerie. I'm not sure what time."

"That's fine. I should be home all day."

He gave her a lovely smile. "Happy birthday, Valerie."

"Thank you, Ed."

As soon as he'd walked out the door, Rhonda hurried to her with some more wrapped cake. She put her hands out and Rhonda put the cake in her hands, and then said, "Don't forget your gift."

She reached over, clasped the gift-wrapped package, and passed it to Valerie.

"*Denke*, Rhonda. It was very thoughtful of you, and thank you again for helping make it such a wonderful night."

Rhonda leaned forward on tiptoes and kissed her on the cheek. "Good night, Valerie. Enjoy the rest of your birthday." Valerie walked out into the cold night air. She was going home to an empty house, and for the first time, she allowed herself to wonder what it would be like to be going home with Ed as a married couple.

Chapter Twenty-Two

Ｔhat night Nancy hardly slept. It annoyed her to see Rhonda continually throwing herself at Ed. Everybody in the community knew that Valerie and Ed were a couple except for Rhonda, it seemed. If Ed wasn't going to tell Valerie how he really felt, then things would have to move forward from Valerie's end. Ed had obviously paid no mind to the conversation they'd had the other day.

Nancy would get them together. She chuckled as she made her husband a breakfast of eggs and bacon. There was nothing she liked more than matching people together. All she wanted was people to be as happy as she and Hezekiah were. She'd matched her older sons and four daughters and they were all so happy. With her last niece, Willow, now married, it was perfect timing for her to concentrate on Ed and Valerie.

Her husband came into the kitchen and sat down. "*Kaffe* ready?"

"*Jah*, here it is." She placed a mug of *kaffe* in front of him.

"*Denke*. What are your plans today?"

"First job of the day is to visit Nerida, and then I'll continue on to Valerie's." To Valerie's to begin the first segment of her plan. She turned back to the frying pan and watched the breakfast cook.

Nancy pushed Nerida's bedroom door open and saw Nerida in bed, half asleep.

Right then, Nerida opened her eyes wide and pushed herself up with her elbows.

"Stay there. You don't have to move."

"I must have been asleep. I didn't even hear you arrive."

"John said he brought a cup of tea up to you and you were asleep." Nancy leaned forward and touched the cup of tea on the nightstand. "It's still quite warm. Do you want to drink it?"

"Okay." Nerida pushed herself up further in the bed and Nancy arranged pillows behind her back before she passed her the tea.

After Nerida had taken a couple of sips of tea, she asked, "How was Valerie's birthday dinner?"

Nancy sat down on the bed next to her. "Well, I was right about Rhonda. She was following Ed around all night and barely left the poor man alone. Valerie barely got a chance to say two words to him."

"But surely if he likes Valerie, he won't change his mind and like Rhonda just because she's chasing him."

"Well, I'd like to think that was the case, but how do we know? And then what will happen to Valerie? She's always liked him."

"I don't think we should interfere."

"Nerida, we're not interfering, not if we're helping them."

"No matter what you call it, it's still the same thing."

Nancy swallowed hard and remembered seeing Ed and Valerie together. They looked like they belonged together. "Anyway, I'm going to Valerie's *haus* soon."

"Well, don't do or say anything to make Rhonda feel uncomfortable. We want her to feel welcome here."

"I quite agree. She's a likable person and she'll fit in well."

"Don't go putting nonsense in Valerie's head."

Nancy frowned at her sister. "Like what?"

"I don't want Valerie to think that she's got to chase after Ed. Just leave things be."

"That's a dramatic turnaround from the other day."

"It's not. Well, if it is, that means I've just had time to think about things these past couple of days. Things turn out like they're meant to."

Nancy wasn't about to argue with her sister again. She would just pretend to agree with her and then do her own thing. "Would you like me to take the tea from you?"

"Please."

Nancy placed the teacup back on the saucer. "Too cold?"

"Just a little."

"I'll make you a fresh cup."

"*Denke*, that would be lovely."

Nancy walked downstairs holding the teacup in the saucer.

When John saw her coming down the stairs, he looked up from his Amish newspaper. "Tea gone cold?"

"*Jah*, I'm making her a fresh cup."

John started to stand.

"Stay there. I can fix it. Who's bringing you dinner tonight?"

He chuckled. "I believe it's Daisy's turn."

"Good. It will do them good to think about people other than themselves."

"*Denke* for organizing everything, Nancy. I think that's what you do best."

Nancy couldn't stop smiling. John knew, too, that she was good at organizing things—events as well as people's lives. "Would you like a cup of hot tea too, John?"

"That would be lovely, *denke*, Nancy."

While Nancy waited for the teakettle to boil, she did her best to clean up the kitchen. If Nerida knew how cluttered her kitchen had become, no one would be able to keep her in bed.

Several minutes later, Nancy gave John his tea and then continued up the stairs with her sister's. "There you are, Nerida. It's piping hot."

"Wunderbaar, denke."

Nancy sat back down on her bed. "No more pains?"

Nerida had just taken a sip of tea, and she placed the teacup down on the saucer. "None so far, and I got to thinking, if I don't have any more pain, why am I still in bed?"

"Because the doctor ordered it." Nancy took the cup and saucer from her and placed them on the nightstand. "And you'd be a fool not to listen to him. We must make sure the *boppli* arrives safe, sound, and healthy."

"I suppose you're right, but it's not easy lying here, staring at the four walls."

"Better here than in a hospital bed."

Nerida sighed. "That's true."

"And if you get out of bed and start doing house-work, that's where you might end up."

"Okay, okay. I get your point."

"Have you had many visitors?"

"I've had a lot, and it helps to pass the day. I heard John just now thanking you for all you've done. I don't know what we would've done without you organizing the girls to bring us meals and help with the work around the *haus*."

"As John said, I'm good at organizing people."

"That's true; you are."

"Can I bring you anything else?"

"*Nee*, I've got everything I need."

Nancy stayed talking to her sister for another hour before she headed to Valerie's house.

When Nancy got to Valerie's, no one answered her knock on the front door, so she walked around the back of the house. There she saw Valerie pinning her wash-ing to the clothesline.

"*Gut mayrie*, Valerie."

Valerie jumped and then smiled at her. "*Gut may-rie*. It's a lovely day, isn't it?"

"It is. It's a perfect drying day with this breeze."

"You're alone?" Valerie asked.

"*Jah*, my guest has gone into town to visit Ed at work."

Valerie raised her eyebrows and made no comment.

"Well, aren't you worried?" Nancy asked, getting right to the point of why she was there.

"What would I have to be worried about?"

"Rhonda, of course. She either doesn't know or doesn't care to know that you and Ed are together."

"But we're not together—not really."

Nancy put her hands on her hips. "Well, don't you think that's something that you need to change?"

Valerie shook her head. "I'm not sure."

"I've come here to make you see sense."

Valerie laughed. "I can't force myself on the man."

"You don't need to do that. You just need to give him a little encouragement."

"I don't think you understand how it is with Ed and me. Anyway, I like living alone."

"I don't believe you, Valerie. You've been in love with Ed for years. Well before you married Dirk."

"And maybe things didn't work out between us back then for a very good reason."

"Such as?" Nancy asked.

"There could be many reasons. Ed and I might not be meant to be more than close friends."

Nancy stepped closer and looked into Valerie's eyes. "Tell me you don't love him."

Valerie opened her mouth to speak and then closed it.

"Just as I thought. You're in love with him. Keep pinning out the washing. Don't mind me." Nancy kept looking around at the rocks dividing the nearby garden bed.

Valerie gathered a wet sheet in her hands. "What are you looking for?"

Nancy picked up a large rock. "Something like this."

"Why are you looking for a rock? Don't you have rocks at your place?"

"*Jah*, I suppose I could've brought one with me."

"What are you going to do with it?"

"This." Nancy moved closer to the house, drew the rock back over her head, and with the force of both hands, threw it at the kitchen window. The window shattered, making a loud crash.

Valerie gasped and dropped the sheet onto the ground. "Why did you do that?" She stared open-mouthed at the window, and then looked at Nancy.

Nancy dusted off her hands. "It's for your own good. You don't have a phone anymore, do you?"

Valerie could only shake her head.

"I'm going home and I'll call Ed to come out and fix your window." Nancy grinned smugly.

"Ed doesn't need a broken window to visit me."

"I know, but I am shocking you into thinking about your future with Ed. While you're waiting for him, think about how you'd feel to lose Ed to Rhonda. And when he arrives, you must tell him how you feel."

"You can't force these things on people, Nancy. Things must happen in their own way."

"How many years has it been since Dirk died?"

"A few."

"And has your relationship with Ed progressed?"

"*Jah*, I think it has."

Nancy shrugged. "I don't think it has. Anyway, I'll pay for the window."

"Oh, I know you will. There was never any question about that." Valerie folded her arms over her chest. "I can't believe you did that! There was no need. It was a perfectly good window."

She'd never heard Valerie speak so harshly to her. "Trust me, Valerie. If you love Ed like I think you do, you need to break down those walls around your heart." Valerie was staring back at her, not saying a word, and Nancy thought it best to leave. "I'll call him right now."

Nancy hurried to her buggy and drove away, hoping she hadn't done something that would ruin their friendship forever. It was a bold move, but she had needed to do something to shock Valerie into telling Ed how she truly felt.

Chapter Twenty-Three

When Nancy got back to her own home, she picked up the phone in the barn and called Ed's place of business. Ed answered the phone. "Ed, it's Nancy Yoder."

"Hello, Nancy. What can I do for you?"

"It's actually for Valerie. She has a broken window at her *haus*."

"Is she hurt?"

"*Nee.* She's fine. It's her kitchen window."

"I'll go there now and take the measurements. How did it break?"

"I'll let her tell you about that."

Ed hung up the phone's receiver. This was a perfect excuse to visit Valerie. Things between them had been awkward at her birthday dinner and he had to tell her why.

He knew Rhonda was on the verge of making her attentions toward him known and that was one thing he feared. That was why he'd been wary when she said she was thinking of moving to Lancaster County, and she wasn't a woman backward in coming forward. Ed could tell from the way Rhonda looked at him, and from the hints she'd dropped, that she thought the two of them should marry.

The only thing he could do was tell Valerie how he felt, how he'd always felt about her. She hadn't picked up on any of the hints he'd dropped about marriage. He'd ask her to marry him and prepare himself for heartbreak if she said no. He'd heard back from others that she'd said she enjoyed living on her own and he could only hope she didn't really mean it.

He told his oldest son where he was heading and walked out the door, placing his hat firmly on his head.

Just as he was climbing into his buggy, a taxi pulled up. He sat and waited for it to leave, so he could move his buggy out of the lot.

"Ed."

He turned to see it had been Rhonda in the taxi.

"Hello, Rhonda."

"Where are you going?"

"Just heading out to measure up a job."

"Can I come too?"

She had the worst timing in the world. "*Nee*, sorry. Not today."

"Oh." Her face fell.

"Have you come to town to do some shopping?"

"I was hoping we could have lunch together."

"I often don't take the time during the workday to eat."

"Oh, Ed, you must eat. You need someone to take care of you." She shook her head. "That's plain to see."

"I've been doing fine by myself."

"How long will you be?"

"I might be some time. It's hard to say with jobs like these."

She narrowed her dark eyes. "What? It takes hours to measure something?"

"Measuring is the most important part of the job. If we measure incorrectly, the glass we cut isn't going to fit and it'll be wasted."

She looked around. "The taxi's already gone. Do you mind taking me into town where the stores are?"

"Sure. I can go that way."

Rhonda smiled and climbed into his buggy, and then Ed maneuvered his horse-drawn buggy onto the road.

He glanced at her. "What's Nancy doing today?"

"She said she was visiting a few people."

"You could've gone with her."

"*Nee*, I think she needs a little bit of time away from me. We see each other all the time. And I am staying there."

"I see what you mean."

"I left early this morning and had breakfast at a little diner. I needed some alone time. I don't mind going out by myself because I don't need constant company all the time."

Ed nodded.

"What about you?" she asked.

He glanced over at her. "What about me, what?"

"Do you like company all the time?"

He chuckled. "I've got a *haus* full of boys and then they have their friends and girlfriends over, and as you know one of them is married, so I always have a crowded *haus*. I never get a chance to be by myself much."

"Where's your job at?"

"Not too far away."

Ed desperately didn't want to tell her that he was going out to Valerie's house. He had that birthday gift to give Valerie and if she was by herself and the time was right, he'd propose. It was Nancy who had made him see things from a woman's point of view. He'd always felt guilty that he hadn't been the one to tell Valerie that he was marrying Rita. For the sake of convenience, he'd pushed it to the back of his mind. From what Nancy said, though, it hadn't been pushed to the back of Valerie's mind.

"Yes, but where?" Rhonda persisted.

"The opposite way from where we're heading now."

"Oh, Ed, I'm sorry to put you out of your way."

He chuckled. "It's not that far out of my way. It doesn't matter. Are things working out well with you staying at Nancy and Hezekiah's?"

"*Jah*. I'm getting on with them very well. Everything is going fine and I'll soon be moved into my new home."

"I'm glad you're happy."

"It's good to be surrounded with people you can call your friends."

"I totally agree."

"I should stop by one night and cook for you and the boys."

"*Nee!*" He glanced at her to see she looked a little shocked. "I mean, the boys aren't often home until very late. Half of them have got girlfriends."

"*Jah*, you'll soon have them all married off and you'll be on your own."

He chuckled. "I'll look forward to the peace and the quiet."

Rhonda stayed silent for a few moments.

Then they came to where the stores were. "Now, where shall I stop and let you out?"

"Anywhere you like and I'll take a walk around and have a look at things."

He glanced over at her and smiled. He liked her enthusiasm and bright manner. Once he'd pulled the buggy over to the side of the road, he said, "How are you getting home?"

"I'll get a taxi."

"Are you sure?"

"Jah."

"I'd offer to collect you, but I don't know how long I'll be."

"That's okay, Ed. You do your work and I'll shop. I need to buy things for my new home."

He chuckled. "Bye, Rhonda."

She got out of the buggy, turned around, and gave him a wave.

The closer Ed got to Valerie's house, the more nervous he became. How would he bring up the subject of why he'd married Rita?

He glanced over at the back seat and saw Valerie's gift still sitting there. He was grateful that Rhonda hadn't seen it. She'd asked enough questions as it was.

When he came to the house, he got down from the buggy, took Valerie's gift out of the back, and made his way to her front door. Just as he had reached the last porch step, she opened the door and stood there smiling.

He held out the gift. "Happy birthday, for yesterday. I know I should have given this to you on your birthday."

She laughed. "*Denke*. But you shouldn't have done it at all."

"It's only something small. It's a teacup and saucer."

"Ed, you shouldn't tell me. Now I won't be surprised when I open it."

He chuckled. "I didn't want you to think it was more."

"That's a lovely gift."

"You haven't opened it yet."

She pulled the end of the red ribbon until it unraveled and then peeled back the paper. On the box was a picture of a pale pink cup with small red flowers. "Oh, Ed, it is so beautiful."

"I'm glad you like it."

"I do."

"Now, where's this broken window?"

"Come inside and I'll show you. It's the kitchen window."

Ed stood in front of the window. "How did it break?"

"Don't ask. There was a real mess on the floor. I've only just finished cleaning it up."

He pulled a tape out of his work-apron pocket and started his measuring, recording the results on a notepad. "I'll need to measure outside as well."

She followed him outside, and once he had finished making his measurements, he said, "I think we should have this finished by the end of the day."

"I'd like it if you could do that."

"Valerie, I need to talk with you about something."

"What is it?"

"Do you have time?"

"Yes, I've got all day. Would you like a cup of tea or *kaffe*?"

He shook his head. "Not for me."

"It's a lovely day; we can sit on the porch."

Ed followed her back to the porch with his heart thumping, hoping things weren't going to backfire on him. He didn't know where to start. Perhaps it was better to leave the past in the past and not mention things that happened long ago.

When they were both seated, she stared at him, waiting for him to begin.

"Marry me, Valerie?" he blurted out.

"You want to marry me?"

The relief he felt over finally asking her the question that had been on his lips for over a year was enormous. "*Jah.* I want to marry you, or I wouldn't have asked you. I've always loved you."

Valerie shook her head and looked away. "Don't say that."

He nodded, understanding completely. "You're thinking about Rita and Dirk?"

"*Jah.*" She slowly nodded.

He sighed.

She screwed up her nose. "Why are you asking me now?"

He frowned. "It's about time. First, before you give me your answer, there's something I have to tell you. I've owed you an explanation for a long time."

"Go on."

"You and I were set to marry and then things went wrong when I went to Lowville to help my *onkel*. I was friendly with Rita, but she was never more than a friend. There was a murder."

"A murder?"

"*Jah*. An *Englischer* ran in front of my buggy as a joke and caused my horse to rear up. The man was from a wealthy family and was well-known in the area. I stopped the buggy and explained that it wasn't a good thing to scare the buggy horses. I wasn't the first one he'd done it to. He picked up a large rock and threw it at me. Then I turned to get back in my buggy and he jumped on me, pulled me to the ground, and started punching me. A crowd gathered, but no one pulled him off me. As you know, we can't strike back."

"I know, of course. So he kept punching you?"

"I blocked the punches the best I could and then after a while he figured I'd suffered enough, so he hurled abuse at me and let me go. I was battered and bloody and so I headed back to the cabin on my *onkel's* farm, where I was staying, to fix myself up."

"No one was there to help?"

"*Nee*, and the next day Rita had heard what happened and she came to the cabin early in the morning to see if I was okay. She bandaged my hands where I had large pieces of skin missing. It wasn't a pretty sight." He held out one hand and pulled up his sleeve. "I've still got scars."

"I didn't know."

"While Rita was still tending my wounds, she told me something shocking and unbelievable."

"What was it?"

"That same man who'd been harassing us and the horses had raped her and she was expecting his child."

"*Nee!*" Valerie held her stomach.

"While I was getting over what she'd told me, there was a knock on the door. It was the police. The man who'd attacked me and raped Rita had been found murdered. Two men had told the police I'd done it. The man had been found hanged on a tree near the place he'd attacked me the day before."

Valerie gasped. "What happened?"

"Rita stepped forward and before I could stop her, she said it couldn't have been me because she was with me the whole night. She gave me an alibi."

"She lied?"

"She did. We were living in a nightmare and to save ourselves, we lied. Otherwise, I might have gone to jail and who knows what would've happened to Rita and her child."

Valerie wiped away a tear. "Poor Rita."

"So I married her. Rita was distraught that if word got out that it was that man's baby, his wealthy family might have taken the baby from her."

Valerie looked out over the swaying grasses of the fields. Now things made sense. This was different from Rhonda's version of Ed and Rita having to get married. Perhaps Rhonda didn't know the truth behind Ed and Rita's story.

Ed continued, "We were in the whole thing together. I didn't know who had killed that man, but I knew it wasn't Rita or me. We married as quickly as the bishop allowed and soon after that, Rita miscarried."

"That's so sad."

"It was, and I felt so bad that you were affected in this whole thing too."

"If you'd told me back then, I would've understood," Valerie said.

"But don't you see, Valerie, this wasn't my story to tell? It involved Rita and I couldn't ask her if I could tell you, the woman I loved. We were married in the sight of *Gott*, and I had to love the woman I was with. You would've been ashamed of me for lying, I knew that too. There was… I just couldn't have told you. I wouldn't have been able to find the words."

"I don't know what I would've thought, but it would've been nice to know that you'd left me for a real reason. I felt so deserted and worthless."

He reached out and took her hand in his. "I'm sorry I made you feel that way."

Valerie nodded, pleased to know the truth.

"That's all of it. I don't know why I didn't tell you before now. I was ashamed for being cowardly and lying, but I was young back then. Now I believe I would do things differently."

"We've all made mistakes in our youth. *Denke* for telling me now. I'm pleased you did. I always thought you'd fallen in love with another woman and forgotten me."

"*Nee*, I never forgot you, but I couldn't let myself love you once I was married. I pushed every thought of you out of my mind. In time, I grew to love Rita, I really did. She was a *gut fraa* and a *wunderbaar mudder*. We had a happy life."

"I feel sad for Rita. She went through quite a bit."

"We had a happy life. The joy of our sons made up for the earlier pain we went through."

Valerie blew out a deep breath. "Does Rhonda know any of this?"

"*Nee*. Only you and I know. Why do you ask?"

"Rhonda let slip that Rita was expecting before you were married and I assumed…"

"Everyone assumed that. Rhonda likes to spread stories, I'm afraid. I didn't tell anyone anything, but people found out Rita was expecting and I'm not certain what Rita told her *schweschder*. Rhonda's a good-hearted woman, and she's been a *gut schweschder*-in-law." He chuckled. "Let people think what they want. It was so long ago it barely matters."

"It still matters to me."

"I know. I meant that it doesn't matter what people think, except for you."

"Did they ever find out who murdered that man?"

"*Jah*. It was those two men who said it was me. They killed their friend. The police caught up with them two years later. They might have gotten away with it if Rita hadn't stepped forward like she did. I might be sitting in a jail cell now if it weren't for Rita giving me an alibi."

"You were there to help each other through difficult times."

"It was hard and when we lost the *boppli*, Rita was convinced it was because she lied to the police. She thought *Gott* was punishing her even though we had both confessed our sin to Him. It was a sad time."

"I can imagine. I've never had a child, but losing one must be…there'd be no words."

Tears brimmed in his eyes. "We both were looking forward to raising that child. He wasn't mine, but he was. He was ours, and to lose him was something so tragic…"

When she saw him blinking rapidly to hold back tears, she squeezed his hand.

He wiped a tear away. "I've had happiness and tragedy, and now I want—all I want—is our time, Valerie. It's our time to be happy."

All Valerie's past hurts and doubts had been washed away with hearing the truth of what had happened all those years ago. "I had no idea you and Rita had been through so much." She smiled at Ed and in her heart, she forgave him for abandoning her all those years ago. "Do you think we might be too old to begin a life together?"

"*Nee.* You're never too old for love. You were the first woman I loved and you'll be the last. Will you marry me, Valerie?"

Valerie nodded. "I would love to marry you, Ed. *Jah*, I will."

"Really?"

"*Jah.*"

"You mean it?" he asked.

She laughed. "I do."

He leaped off his chair and pulled her up into his arms. Then his arms fell from around her waist and he grabbed both of her hands. "We must tell everyone."

"The bishop first," she said.

"I'd like us to marry as soon as we can. I don't want any more time to be wasted."

She nodded and blinked to stop the tears that were threatening to fall. "I'd like that, too."

He pulled her into his arms once more and she rested her head on his shoulder. This was finally going to happen after all. She was going to marry the man she'd loved for so long.

Chapter Twenty-Four

On the morning of her wedding, Valerie drank the last cup of hot tea she'd ever have at her kitchen table. In a little over an hour, she would be Mrs. Bontrager.

Ed had bought them a new home, saying, *New home, new memories*. A much-appreciated romantic gesture from the man Valerie thought hadn't a romantic bone in his body.

The wedding was taking place at their new home. Everyone was there right now getting everything ready. The ladies were organizing the food, the men were filling the house with long wooden benches for the ceremony, and Ed would be instructing the men in what to do and where everything should be placed. Ed had an eye for detail and liked everything just so.

Surprisingly, it was Rhonda who'd insisted on driving Valerie from her old house to her new one for the wedding. Ed's sister-in-law had taken it with grace that Valerie and Ed were to be married. Rhonda had become a friend, rather than taking Valerie's place, as Valerie had once feared.

Valerie looked around the kitchen. Over the next few

days, she would have to ready her house so it could be leased. Since Ed still had some of his boys living at home, he'd decided that the boys should continue to live there and the family's house was staying as is. She thought Ed was hoping one of his sons might want to buy the house one day.

Now Valerie had a nice new home that she could do with as she wished. Marrying Ed meant she wouldn't have to struggle financially as she'd been doing since Dirk's death. Even though she was sad to leave her home, she was excited to be moving on to something else—another chapter in her life and, she hoped, a happier one.

Valerie brought her cup to the sink and rinsed it in hot running water before leaving it to dry by the sink. After she had wiped her hands on a towel, she smoothed down her carefully-sewn blue wedding dress. On hearing a buggy, she moved into the living room. A quick look out the window confirmed it was Rhonda. She straightened her prayer *kapp*, smoothing back some loose strands of hair.

Instead of knocking on the door, Rhonda opened it and walked right on in. Her face lit up when she saw Valerie. "You're so beautiful."

"*Denke*, Rhonda. I feel beautiful today."

"You should. I can't think of two nicer people to marry each other." She sighed, exhaling deeply. "My two good friends are getting married."

"That's a lovely thing to say."

"It's true."

Valerie giggled like a girl. She found that she felt like a young girl today. This had been her dream as a young woman, to marry Ed, and after many eventful years, that dream was finally about to become real.

"Will you miss this *haus*?"

"I was just thinking that. I will, but it's exciting to have a new place to start our life together."

"We should leave now."

Valerie stepped forward. "I'm ready."

"Your apron and cape?"

Valerie looked down at herself and laughed. "My head's in a muddle. I don't know where they are."

Rhonda pointed to the couch. "Is that them?"

Valerie laughed again as she headed to them. "That's them all right." She quickly donned the apron, putting on the cape while following Rhonda out the door. When she stepped out, she looked up at the house, and then turned away. Today, so many changes would take place. She would gain a new husband and live in a new place. It was a lot to take in.

Valerie traveled to her wedding with Rhonda chattering in her ear. She was too nervous to concentrate on anything Rhonda said.

"Here we are," Rhonda announced. "You get out here and I'll park the buggy."

"*Denke*, Rhonda."

Valerie got down from the buggy and headed to the house.

Ed stepped out to meet her, grinning from ear-to-ear. "It's finally about to happen," he said.

"I know. I'm so happy." He'd never looked more handsome than in the dark suit and bowtie she'd made him.

"That's all I want. I just want you to be happy." His eyes swept over her. "You look so beautiful."

"Denke."

"We'll put our past behind us and have a future to-gether."

"I'd like nothing more," Valerie said.

Hand-in-hand, they walked into the house. They stood in front of the bishop and everyone quickly took their seats.

The bishop cleared his throat, and said, "It's been a long time coming, but I think we all knew this day was going to happen."

There was a rumble of laughter through the crowd.

Ed and Valerie looked at each other and smiled. The bishop rarely made remarks like that.

After a prayer, a hymn, and a short talk from the bishop, Valerie and Ed were pronounced married. They gave each other a special smile and Valerie couldn't wait for their very first kiss that would take place later that night, once all their guests had left.

Ed guided Valerie out of the house and into the cov-ered area at the back of the house where they would have the meal. Some of the ladies had already made a start on spreading the food onto the tables. And there was always plenty of food at an Amish wedding. There was the special fried chicken, which was Ed's favor-ite, along with lamb and other roasted meats. Plenty of mashed potatoes and coleslaw, vegetable dishes, bolo-gna, and creamed celery were spread out.

The women had made several wedding cakes and the desserts—fruit pies, puddings, and doughnuts— were just as varied and plentiful as the main meal.

Even though they hadn't given people much notice of their wedding, there were still hundreds of guests in attendance.

Valerie was overwhelmed with gratitude to God for finally answering her many prayers to be united with the man she loved. It had taken a long time, and when he'd married Rita, she'd had to abandon that hope.

"*Denke* for marrying me," Ed said as they both sat down at the head wedding table.

"*Denke* for asking me."

"I shouldn't have taken so long."

"Everything has worked out for the best."

He nodded. "I'm just so sad I hurt you in the way that I did."

"All is forgotten. I forgot it as soon as you told me what happened."

"I'll put it behind me. I'll spend the rest of my life making you happy."

Valerie knew this was perfect. Ed was the only man for her and always had been. "I just feel this is how it always should have been from the start."

He chuckled. "I've learned never to take love for granted. I should've asked you a lot sooner than I did."

"No more regrets. We're married now."

He leaned close and whispered, "I want to take you in my arms and kiss you like you've never been kissed."

Valerie gave a giggle. "We have to wait until everyone leaves."

"I'll be counting every single minute."

"Me too."

Valerie and Ed temporarily put aside their longing to be alone and enjoyed their wedding day with family and friends, old and new.

Throughout the festivities of the day, there was one special person missing. That person was Nerida, who was still on bed rest.

Weeks later.

Because of her difficult pregnancy, Nerida had made the choice to have her baby in the hospital with her midwife present. That way, the doctors would be there in case there were complications.

Her baby arrived after a six-hour labor. John returned to Nerida's side after he'd called everyone on his list to tell them they'd had a healthy baby girl.

Nerida stared down at the tiny baby girl in her arms. Nancy had been there for every minute of the labor.

"What are you going to call her?" Nancy asked.

Nerida glanced up at her husband, who was right by her side. "We decided to call her Alyssa."

"Is that a flower name?"

John chuckled. "I'm not sure, but I think there's a flower called Alyssium, or a group of flowers with that name."

"So what if it's not a flower name? It's close to a flower name, and we like it."

"I don't care about all that anymore, Nerida. Name your *boppli* whatever you'd like."

"That's very generous of you, Nancy," John said.

Nancy glanced up at John, wondering if she detected a hint of sarcasm in his voice. Why would he say that was generous of her? Maybe he was just being polite.

Nerida glanced up at her husband. "We've got a healthy baby girl."

He nodded. "*Gott* has blessed us with another *dochder.* Just when we thought we were going to have an empty *haus*, *Gott* once more filled it."

Nancy looked around and saw that the midwife had stepped out. Now was a chance for John and Nerida to be on their own, since Nancy had been there for the last few hours. "I'll leave you two alone for a while. Or, I should say, 'you three.' I'll just be outside. I might go to the cafeteria to have a cup of *kaffe*."

"*Denke*, Nancy," John said.

Nancy nodded and took one more look at the tiny baby, and then she kissed her younger sister on the forehead before leaving the room.

As Nancy sat in the cafeteria drinking a cup of coffee that tasted as bad as she thought dishwater might, she looked out the window at the sky.

She mused on how life changes over a short period of time.

Only a few years ago, Nerida and she weren't talking and hadn't talked for many years. Now they were the best of friends, Nerida's two daughters were married, and Nerida even had a new baby.

What would've happened to Willow and Violet if her sister hadn't made amends with her? Nancy knew that it was due to her that Willow and Violet had made such happy marriages.

Nancy sighed and pushed the coffee cup away from her. Then there was the recently married Ed and Valerie. They never would've gotten together if it hadn't been for her. Nancy gave a silent giggle about breaking Valerie's kitchen window. That had shocked her into something, it seemed.

She didn't know whether it was the sleepless night helping Nerida through the labor or what, but tears started to form in her eyes. God had given her so many gifts. Her family had been a blessing. Her two sons and her four daughters were all married, and she had grandchildren now with more still arriving. She'd gently guided each child into choosing the proper spouse, and God had blessed each and every one of them.

"Are you ready to go home?" a deep voice said from behind her, causing her to jump.

She looked around to see Hezekiah. "What are you doing here?"

He sat down at the table next to her. "I'm here because I missed you dreadfully last night."

Nancy's heart filled with gladness. He'd not said anything like that for an awfully long time. "You missed me?"

He nodded.

"And you came all this way just to tell me this?"

"I did."

Nancy chuckled. "Have you seen your new niece?"

"Not yet. I'm guessing she looks and sounds the same as any other *boppli*. Small and with a loud yowl."

Nancy shook her head at her husband pretending he wasn't potty over babies. "I'll take you to see her and then we can go home."

He reached out and took her hand. "I love you, Nancy Yoder."

Nancy gasped and looked around, slightly embarrassed that someone might have heard. "Hezekiah."

He continued to look at her, seemingly not caring who might have heard. "I do."

She smiled. "I'll have to stay away more often."

"*Nee*, I won't let you. Never again." He stood and pulled her to her feet. "Let's go home." On their way out of the cafeteria, he asked the important question, "What did they call the *boppli*?"

"Alyssa."

"That's a nice name."

"*Jah*. I think they like that name because it's close to a flower name."

"And you're not mad about that?" he asked quietly, almost timidly.

"Of course not. Why would I be?"

* * * * *

"Dating is so complicated."

"People are complicated, Noah. Every single person you meet is dealing with something."

He asked, "How did you get so wise?"

"Never said I was."

"I'm being serious. How did you learn to navigate so seamlessly through these kinds of interactions, and why aren't you married?"

Olivia Mae thought her eyes were going to pop out of her head. "Did you really just ask me that?"

"I did."

"A little intrusive."

"Meaning you don't want to answer?"

"Meaning it's none of your business."

"Fair enough, though it's like asking a horse salesman why he doesn't own a horse."

"My family situation is…unique."

"You mean with your grandparents?"

She nodded instead of answering.

"I've got it." Noah resettled his hat, looking quite pleased with himself.

"Got what?"

"The solution to my dating disasters."

He leaned forward, close enough that she could smell the shampoo he'd used that morning.

"You need to give me dating lessons."

"What do you mean?"

"You and me. We'll go on a few dates…say, three. You can learn how to do anything if you do it three times."

"That's a ridiculous suggestion."

"Why? I learn better from doing."

"Do you?"

"I've already learned not to take a girl to a gas station, but who knows how many more dating traps are waiting for me."

"So this would be…a learning experience."

"It's a perfect solution." He tugged on her *kapp* string, something no one had done to her since she'd been a young teen.

"I can tell by the shock on your face that I've made you uncomfortable. It's a *gut* idea, though. We'd keep it businesslike—nothing personal."

Olivia Mae had no idea why the thought of sitting through three dates with Noah Graber made her stomach twirl like she'd been on a merry-go-round. Maybe she was catching a stomach bug.

"Wait a minute. Are you trying to get out of your third date? Because you promised your *mamm* that you would give this thing three solid attempts."

"And I'll keep my word on that," Noah assured her. "After you've tutored me, you can throw another poor unsuspecting girl my way."

Olivia Mae stood, brushed off the back of her dress and pointed a finger at Noah, who still sat in the grass as if he didn't have a care in the world.

"All right. I'll do it."

Don't miss
A Perfect Amish Match *by Vannetta Chapman,*
available May 2019 wherever
Love Inspired® books and ebooks are sold.

www.LoveInspired.com

Looking for inspiration in tales
of hope, faith and heartfelt romance?

Check out **Love Inspired**® and
Love Inspired® **Suspense** books!

New books available every month!

CONNECT WITH US AT:

Facebook.com/groups/HarlequinConnection

 Facebook.com/HarlequinBooks

 Twitter.com/HarlequinBooks

 Instagram.com/HarlequinBooks

 Pinterest.com/HarlequinBooks

ReaderService.com

LIGENRE2018R2